Bob,
Love You Sweet
Cousin....
Debbie

D French
2019

CRYSTAL SKY

DJ French

Edited by Lindsey Kolish

All characters are fiction

© 2016 DJ French All rights reserved. No part of this publication may be reproduced, distributed, or transmitted in any form or by any means, including photocopying, recording, or other electronic or mechanical methods, without the prior written permission of the publisher, except in the case of brief quotations embodied in critical reviews and certain other noncommercial uses permitted by copyright law. ISBN (Print) 978-1-48358-727-1 (Ebook) 978-1-48358-728-8

Dedicated to my kids, Matt, Randi, Jenna and Emily

INTRODUCTION

In the hills that begin at the foot of the Ozark Mountains lives a woman. She has resided there since 1972, when she was just a child. Her story was never fully accepted by the practical and skeptical minds of that era. It was treated like a fable, a concoction of someone's imagination.

At first her claims were questioned, understandably, for they were as bizarre and randomly rare as a UFO sighting.

Few people actually witnessed her dreams unfold into horrible nightmares during daylight. She was real, the things that were observed and documented happened.

The legend goes that she was in possession of some kind of supernatural ability, which manifested into colorful visions. It was as if she had a third eye in her mind.

Unexplainable as it sounds, it was believed that just as a child is born with a genius brain, he or she could also be gifted with psychic abilities.

A clearer example could be made of a child prodigy that excels very quickly in playing the piano. The studied composers and conductors sit with mouths agape. It is beyond their comprehension and they are in awe of these tiny tots as they master the works of Mozart. The youngest one reported was barely two and a half years old.

These children exist. That's what this story is about, the actual existence of a little girl who was able to see upcoming events before they happened. She has resided in the same place for over forty years surrounded by quiet hills and valleys. Her name is Skyler Conrad.

At two years old, Skyler's grandmother, Rose, noticed something unusual with Skyler's eyes. The pediatrician referred her to an optometrist to take a closer look.

While conducting a special scan, the optician became quite astonished with a particularly bright ray of light that was not supposed to be there. The tiny light located deep in the cornea, was floating directly behind the retina. There was no logical reason for it to be lit. He repeated the scan several times, and while the beam moved, it did not dissipate. When he finally admitted he was stumped, he shared the scans with his fellow opticians. Unable to find a plausible explanation, they were in a quandary as to what to do about the unusual case. They concluded it was an anomaly and everything was written down tidily in her record.

The word anomaly literally means, not normal. This is why her story needs to be told; there are no other cases like Skyler's. The events described here are taken from a journal kept by Rose England.

In addition to being Skyler's grandmother, she was a woman of God. As an Ordained Minister, Rose accepted miracles, and eventually she accepted supernatural visions. This was happening to her precious granddaughter.

Skyler's condition was observed and recorded resulting in pages of documentation, but it has all been filed away for decades. No one has ever been able to interview her until now. It's the year 2013, and she lives alone. She has become a recluse, choosing to live a life of obscurity in the hills, behind a locked gate.

I've been given permission to write all of this down, and to explain a story that is unexplainable.

The questions are:

Can one see a fated event with his or her eyes closed, and could something or someone unknown be watching to give warning?

1
Big Brother Bo

Today they were going to a halfway house to see their dad for the first time in eight years. There wasn't any light in the room as Bo shook his sister awake, so he went over to the window and pulled open the curtains.

"Stop it, Leave me alone." She was tired. Her arm partially covered her eyes, and he could just barely see their glimmer in the filtered light that streamed in through the open shades.

"I said it's time to wake up, Sky. Come on, we have a really important day today. I need you to wake up now."

Bo had watched over her since she was born. He was six years old when his grandmother first laid her in his arms. His skinny legs hung off of the tiny sofa in the hospital room. He looked her over, gazing at her tiny bud shaped mouth moving in a suckling motion.

He loved her immediately and felt the need to protect her, kissing her on her tiny head, he held her for as long as they let him.

Her name was Skyler Marie Conrad. Her dark lashes fringed bright icicle blue eyes, which resembled the reflection of a clear winter day. Their unusual shade inspired her name, which they occasionally shortened to Sky.

When Skyler was a baby, Bo went directly into the nursery everyday after school. He would dress her and take her out in her pink stroller. The adoration was mutual, her little legs would start kicking and she'd reach her tiny arms toward him as he stood over her. For two years he'd wished for a baby brother or sister and she was finally here. Some mornings, his mother would come into his bedroom to find her all tucked in with him.

There wasn't anything Bo loved more than playing with her and making her laugh. His favorite thing to do was to swing her in her little jumpy swing. As he pushed her back and forth she stared at him, he was content to just watch her eyes light up. She was his…and he would often help feed her and bathe her.

Their father, Jimmy, was not so attentive. He'd gone off the beaten path and straight down the river with his addictive behavior. He chased fast money and the fastest way to get it, was dealing dope.

It was just a matter of time until the day he would get arrested; that day came when Bo was seven and Skyler was twenty months old.

From a very young age, Jimmy had a penchant for getting into trouble. When he was barely sixteen, he'd broken into a gun shop, stealing eight guns. They all showed up at pawnshops in the surrounding area. Jimmy was not charged because he was a juvenile. A lawyer got him off with just a slap on the wrist and a few nights in lock-up.

He swore to everyone he'd learned his lesson and got a steady job. He was witty and cheerful, everyone liked him and he woke up everyday and went to work. The drug use was well hidden, but Jimmy was an addict. Rose knew something was wrong and had misgivings when Bo was born. She wasn't sure if Jimmy had what it took to be a good father, but she held on to the hope that he did.

Now, six years later, Jimmy had gotten stopped on highway 44 with two kilos of cocaine in the trunk. It was found hidden in a suitcase, underneath a stack of clothes. He was in deep trouble and even the fact that Rose offered to bond him out didn't help, this was a trafficking conviction. The judge threw the book at him and he was sentenced to ten years hard time.

Annie Mae England was Rose's only child. Headstrong and beautiful, she would go north if her mother asked her to go south. That was just the way she was. The day she turned 18, she told her mother she was moving out and that's exactly what she did. She moved in with Jimmy.

She was barely twenty when Bo was born. Playing house, the young couple was in love and Bo was a good baby. They worked at getting ahead, but they were always preoccupied with the next party.

There was a revolving door of people in and out of their little nest, with a new face on the sofa every weekend. Baby Bo had his own room at his grandmother's, she was often the one tucking him in and reading him stories.

For the first few years of Bo's young life, Annie had her foot halfway in and halfway out of her mother, Rose's house. As she landed on the doorstep with a suitcase, she told Rose she felt the walls closing in and Jimmy wasn't around anyway. Then, she would do an about face and return to the apartment she shared with him.

By the time Skyler was born, they weren't getting along. Jimmy's job at the 7-11 wasn't bringing in enough money, so Annie got a job to help keep soup and crackers in the house. When Skyler was just six weeks old, Annie plopped both kids down at her moms to attend some outdoor festival. Jimmy was waiting out in the car and when Annie took too long, he laid on the horn.

Rose was disappointed in them as the bills went unpaid. The kids were often sick with colds and ear infections and Annie didn't have proper medicine. Their grandmother would just bundle them up and go to the drugstore, purchasing Tylenol and anything else she needed to tend to a runny nose. Jimmy and Annie never realized what it meant to take care of kids, or themselves for that matter.

They'd really blown it, and now after seven years together and two kids, Jimmy was heading to prison. Annie was stubborn at first and wanted to stay independent, so she kept the apartment. Two little ones and a steady babysitter were a lot for a vibrant young woman to handle alone. She took on another job, bartending at a local watering hole.

A month had gone by and Annie was determined to make it alone without her mothers help. Skyler stood crying in her crib. She was wet, and a bottle needed to be warmed. Dinner hadn't been prepared and now, it was bed and bath time for the kids. Bo just stood there as the thirteen year-old babysitter talked on the phone. He was watching his life unravel like a loosely wrapped ball of string. He called his grandmother.

"Grandma, I'm hungry and Skyler won't stop crying."

"Where's your mom, Bo?"

"She's at work. Maggie's talking on the phone and I told her we need dinner." It was eight o'clock at night and Rose felt frustrated. At seven years old, Bo realized something wasn't right.

"I'll be there in ten minutes, Bo."

Rose came right away, paid the babysitter, packed some clothes, and took the kids to her house.

Annie called her mom, livid. "You have no right, Mom! They're my kids."

"I know Annie, but the babysitter didn't get them any dinner. I need you to consider leaving them here for good. I can get a nanny and Bo can go to a real good school. You should move home for a while as well, Honey. Let me help you please? Will you at least think about it?"

The next day, Annie announced she was leaving town for a while. She was going to stay with some friends in Illinois while she tried to get some money together. She took everything that was Jimmy's out of the apartment, and put it in an old shed her mom had on the property. The rest she dropped off at the Goodwill.

Annie was restless and young. She knew it was the best thing for the kids to be with Rose. She needed to get away, spread her wings for a couple days. She hadn't handled anything well and she missed Jimmy. Diapers, spit up, and bottles just depressed her, but she didn't tell her mom that. She told her she was sorry, and she would come see the kids every weekend. She loaded up her car, and drove away, leaving them behind, waving good-bye.

After three weeks there was still no word from Annie. The kids jumped if the phone rang, expecting her voice to be heard on the other end. She hadn't called; they didn't know where she was or how she was faring. She'd just disappeared.

Rose England wasn't taken by surprise at her daughter's departure. It seemed like there was always drama with Annie, so Rose did what she'd always done; picked up the pieces from her messes and moved on.

The day Jimmy went to prison was a good day in her mind because the kids were permanently out of that disheveled environment. She prayed for Jimmy, that he'd be safe. She'd find Annie, but for now the kids would get the stability they deserved.

They were her world and she thanked God she had the means to take care of them.

2

Rose England

Rose worried about Annie, but she knew her daughter was a perfect extension of herself. There was a strong chord of strength running through Annie and it was only going to get stronger. She thought about the day her daughter was born. It was a miraculous day, one of the best days of her life. As she reminisced on those years and the feelings of new motherhood she was reminded of Cory. It was too bad he hadn't shared her feelings of wonder.

She was working at the restaurant; she remembered it was a balmy summer evening. The guy in booth 4 kept waving Rose over to his table. On his third glass of sweet tea, he seemed to be awfully thirsty.

He started talking to her. "You know, I might develop borderline diabetes if you won't sit down a minute to chat with me. I've been guzzling this stuff down just so you'd have to come back over to give me a fill-up. Oh, refills are free right?"

She laughed at him. "That is the most bizarre pick-up line I've ever heard. I'll have a minute here as soon as my relief starts. What's your name?"

"Cory, Cory Lucas. I'm not from around here, but I'll be in town awhile." He glanced at her nametag again, making sure he was reading it right. "What time are you off the clock, Ms. Rose?"

"I knock off at six, why?"

"Well, I was hoping to go over to the honky tonk and shake a leg, what do you say? Would you like to show me around?"

"I'll think about it, Cory. Now do me a favor; switch to water, I don't want to be the reason you develop sugar diabetes."

He grinned at her, and said, "It's a deal if you'll go out with me tonight." She studied him a moment, assessing the danger factor. Mentally priding herself on judging character, she nodded her head.

"Meet me here at seven-thirty and you can follow me. We'll go over to Louie's, they have a real good crowd on a Friday night."

"Deal, pretty lady." He was grinning from ear to ear.

Cory left; leaving a smiley face on the bottom of the check, next to a notation that said 7:30. Rose finished her shift in a daze, barely registering the faces of her remaining customers. She was hoping she didn't regret her impetuous decision to go out with this good-looking stranger.

They settled on a table near the back of the establishment, with a good view of the stage. Rose was excited. She had hurriedly showered and put on fresh makeup.

This wasn't her first time here, but she hadn't been on a date in over a year. It wasn't a priority; she was struggling to get her degree in accounting right now. Money was tight and after counting her tips, she clipped coupons on the weekends, choosing to read and turn in early, while her friends went dancing.

"So, what are you doing here in Eureka, Cory?" she asked.

"We've got races this weekend down at South track in Fenton. Have you ever gone?"

"No, I can't say that I have, it sounds very exciting." She was intrigued, never having met a racecar driver before. She needed to stay cool. He was very attractive.

"We're staying at a motel here in town. I'm sure glad I decided to go to Denny's this morning." He was being so direct with his gaze. She felt him moving closer to her, and their legs were almost touching. Rose felt warmth emanating from him. She moved slightly, creating airflow under the table.

"You're really gorgeous, you know?" He'd been listening to her talk, but all of a sudden it was just his voice and his closeness. Rose got skittish as he made her blush.

"Whoa there, Cowboy. Let's just keep it casual and get to know each other for a minute okay? "

"Deal," he said, backing off a little as the tense moment passed.

The music started and they had a wonderful time, the beer was cold and Rose was thirsty. When the dance floor started to tilt, it was time to call it a night. Cory escorted Rose to her car, but she wasn't in any shape to drive. She went to his place to sleep it off on the comfy sofa.

He'd been a complete gentleman, and now he was dropping her off at her car. She was a bit ashamed of drinking too much, but he just laughed it off. He asked to see her for dinner that evening. She said, "Sure." This time she told him where to pick her up.

She dressed with care. As she finished her hair, she looked in the mirror and saw a glow on her cheek; he'd put it there, with his warm gaze. They had dinner at The Silver Spur, the best steak house in town. Full and feeling relaxed from the excellent wine, they headed back to his place to get more acquainted.

"I feel like a teenager." Rose had kicked off her shoes and was singing to Rod Steward at the top of her lungs. "Wake up, Maggie I think I got something to say to you." He was making her feel wonderful and she wanted it to continue. That night, after sitting out on the balcony listening to classic soft rock and dancing intimately, Rose fell in love with Cory Lucas. He was patient and tender with her.

Annie was conceived very soon after and Rose was thrilled. She stood looking at the test, seeing a tiny blue symbol and mentally noted it was in the shape of a cross. As she looked in the mirror there was a small tear rolling down her cheek and she felt blessed. She would love this child, and tonight she had to tell Cory.

When Rose was nineteen, she'd been diagnosed with a very rare form of endometriosis that would grow into every space and fill it, leaving no room for conception. That evening after work, she drove to the track to watch the race. She was so excited and as he came over to her after his run, she told him she had a surprise for him.

Later in his room, they had pizza and he reached over softly wiping a bit of sauce off of her cheek.

"Well, what's my surprise Rosie?" He was waiting. She smiled at his pet name for her. No one else called her that, only him. She took a deep breath and let the words tumble out, "I'm pregnant, Cory." She broke the news to her lover and waited for his response. It didn't go well. He seemed stunned and when he didn't smile, she knew he wasn't happy.

"I don't know what to say, I thought you told me you couldn't have children." He drew away slightly, leaning back against the wall. His face had grown ashen, and he was avoiding her gaze. She was hurt, but she tried to explain.

"You don't understand, Cory, it's a miracle." Tears were flowing down Rose's face. She'd only known him twenty-eight days, but she loved him.

"I can't commit to staying here, Rose. You know that, I told you we move around in a circuit all year, it's what I do. God, Rose, I'll be leaving in a week." She put her hand on his arm and said, "It's okay, I'm keeping it and I have no expectations of you at this point. I want this child, I hope you understand."

The race eventually took him away from the pending birth of his baby girl, and he told Rose to kiss her for him, but he wasn't there. He sent her money every month, but he wasn't coming back. His passion was the track and how he could conquer it. Rose raised Annie alone.

Cory did come around every couple of years to visit. When Annie was thirteen years old, he told her he was going to buy her a car someday. She called him a few days after she turned sixteen to ask him if he was going to honor his promise. He didn't answer, but a few weeks later he did call back. He told her, he was coming through town soon and they would talk about it then.

They never heard from him, he'd skipped out on both of them and four years went by before Rose saw him again. Annie was twenty years old, and she'd just had Bo. Annie told him to go take a hike and not to bother contacting her again. He remained a father to her in a biological sense only. He was a stranger to them all.

Rose threw herself into her work and thought about her future. She'd felt a strong call to the pulpit when she was very young, but never acted on it. Her father was a Baptist Minister and Rose would watch him write his sermons. Sometimes, he would bounce them off of her, asking her advice. Rose was proud of her father. Sometimes when the church was empty, she would pull over a stool and stand at the pulpit pretending she was the reverend.

While raising Annie, she began studying for her ordination in the seminary. She would be just like her father. He'd passed away when she was just sixteen, but she knew he would approve. Rose's mother had passed away the year after Annie was born. She would've told Rose to follow her destiny, so that's exactly what she did.

The seminary gave Rose the tools she needed and now her life was a busy one. She had something special as she stood on stage, and the seats were always full. A sea of faces hung on her every word needing the messages she prepared lovingly for them. It was her calling and she had an ability to be so honest and real that folks thought of her as a friend.

As she traveled to engagements and special conventions for women of faith, they clamored for her to return, feeding their hunger by buying her books. The book sales alone had made Rose England very wealthy.

She used her gift to glorify the Lord in heaven, but the two kids were her priority, her center. At 57 years old she reveled in the industrious lifestyle she lived. She loved traveling, and the world was full of destinations she kept in her journals.

Her private life was diligently protected. She lived out in the country, in the hills of Missouri. This sanctuary was her nest, and her safe place to fall. Here, she raised Bo and Sky. The neighbors called it a compound because of the sprawling gates and winding drive that lead to her 6500 square foot home. A massive garage held several cars, and on the two acre lake there was a gazebo and several watercrafts.

There weren't many reasons to leave. With a tennis court, in-ground swimming pool, dirt bikes and four-wheelers, the kids were always outdoors. A cat and two little dogs finished up their family. The home and grounds were protected with high tech surveillance and encompassing it all was an eight-foot tall wrought iron fence.

Rose had become a very well known woman. She was the Pastor of her very own church now, and was recognized everywhere she went. The popularity made her uneasy, her family was safe within the walls of the twenty-five acre property, but once beyond the gates, Rose felt they could be vulnerable somehow. She always knew where the kids were and whom they were with.

She had a letter from Jimmy that said he was up for parole soon. Deep inside Rose feared he would just show up in their lives and take the kids away from her. She couldn't let that happen. They were healthy and happy here, leading normal lives.

Rose forgave her daughter Annie for her frailties, and the fact that her character held little gumption. She likened her to a sapling in a great forest, although her roots were strong, she was blown into a whipped mess from the winds she allowed to blow on her. Her mother's home was a place where Annie felt jailed, so she chose to stay in the unprotected gales. Rose was worried when Annie didn't call, but she concentrated on the children and making sure they were well.

She was especially let down by Jimmy. He was given a gift in these two little people, and he should have been able to rise to the occasion and provide for them. She wished he'd been strong enough to maintain a home for his kids.

After Jimmy went to prison and Annie ran off, Rose hired a private detective to search for her. She needed to know her daughter was safe. It took two weeks, but she was located. She was found in Sauget, Illinois.

The photographs told a story of a twenty-seven year old young woman, living a hedonistic lifestyle. She was smoking, drinking and stripping in some club called Slinky's. The detective brought back an address, a vehicle plate number, as well as a photo of her brand new Illinois driver's license.

Rose contacted her through a letter. She asked Annie to call her every couple of weeks or so, to let her know she was okay. She put two $100 dollar bills in the envelope, telling her that a phone call was thanks enough.

Annie was never going to change. She'd called Rose finally, showing such little concern for the welfare of her own kids that the conversation ended after a brief "How are you?"

Her daughter gushed about how she'd met a real nice guy, and was in the process of finding herself. It was a one sided conversation, and as Rose waited for her to say she loved her kids; it occurred to her that her only child was just a selfish fool. She sent the papers she had prepared for guardianship of both kids. They came back signed, and it broke her heart. She wondered to herself how her little girl was ever going to get back on a healthy path now.

She studied the pictures. Annie had started to let her self go. Her teeth were yellowing and her hair needed a trim. It was surprising, because she'd been a Prom Queen, and even won a local beauty contest.

The kids were taken to the doctor and dentist, and helped with homework. She went to Parent/Teacher meetings and ran them around to get school supplies every year. She'd hired Carla the housekeeper/nanny, to help with raising them. Carla filled in the blanks when Rose was traveling. It worked, and everything flowed well in the household.

Skyler had developed sensitivity to light, and was instructed to seek shade whenever possible. Rose made sure she visited the optometrist regularly. Everyone commented on her bright eyes, which seemed to be lit from within. Rose never thought anything of it. She was used to the beauty of both children. She would soon learn just how incredible Skyler's eyes were.

The two kids were thriving. They would do all kinds of activities together, like taking the rowboat out on the lake. Bo got a job bagging at the local grocery store in town. A junior in high school, he was just a normal kid. He had a ton of friends and they attended all the football games.

He and Sky were driven to school every day by Carla. She was always there, cooking, shopping and chauffeuring. She lived at the house with them, and she loved them.

Bo accompanied Sky to her events as if he were her bodyguard. She was the envy of all of her friends as they teased her saying; "We wish we had a big brother that waited for us at gymnastics and choir. He must really like you, Skyler."

She just smiled, because Bo was not only her brother, he was her best friend and she knew she was lucky. Sometimes they would irritate each other, but Bo had taught her how to drive the four-wheeler and catch a fish in the lake. Their relationship was so close that Skyler never felt she needed a dad. She never felt like she needed a mom either. Rose and Bo were all she needed.

3
Jimmy

At sixteen, Bo was looking forward to learning how to drive a car. Skyler was a tender ten year old that carried her teacup Chihuahua, Matilda, around with her in a pink and black leopard print bag. Eight years had gone by since Jimmy went to prison and today was the day they were going to see him.

Rose sat them down a week ago to tell them the news. Their Dad was out of prison and wanted her to bring the kids for a visit. She asked each one how they felt about going to visit him two hours away.

It took a few minutes for Bo to decide. He turned to his sister, searching her face. She looked worried, confused and was watching his reaction. He felt pretty nervous about it, but was more worried about her being afraid. "What do you think, Sky?" Bo asked her.

"I don't know. I guess we can visit him," she answered. "I wonder what he looks like, and if he's a nice person, I don't remember him at all." She hugged Matilda tighter to her breast, kissing the dog's tiny head. "What do you think, Matilda? Should we go see my dad?" She laughed when the dog let out a little sneeze, as if answering her question.

Both kids told their grandmother they would be on board with a visit.

Rose was a nervous wreck, but she had consented to take the kids to see Jimmy at a halfway house in Belleville, IL. They were going to bring food from a Jack-In-the-Box, and have a picnic in the yard. Jimmy was not allowed to leave, unless it was to work.

Visiting day arrived. Skyler came downstairs and sat at the breakfast bar. She was eating a banana when it suddenly occurred to her that she was going to see her dad today for the first time. She was only a baby when he left, she didn't remember him at all.

Rose came in telling her to take both dogs outside and feed them, and then feed Cleo, the family cat. She obeyed. As she did her chores she thought about what it was going to be like to see her dad. Strange, that's what. It was just going to be strange. She tried to think good thoughts about it.

They set out on their trip and turned on the radio, singing songs and chatting. The kids were starting to feel nervous and their apprehension grew with each mile closer to the meeting with their father. To Sky, he would be a stranger, but Bo remembered things. The small time elapsed memories played like short videos in his mind. They weren't bad, just vague.

Rose studied them in the rearview mirror of her black Mercedes Benz as she drove. She asked if they were nervous or excited. It was definitely not something they were prepared for. There had only been a scattering of correspondence from Jimmy to his kids over the last eight years.

"I just hope Dad is going to be a good guy now," said Sky in her quiet little voice. "Do you think he will like us?" she asked her grandmother.

Rose answered with as much honesty as she could while still conveying a positive outlook. She said, "I bet he will try as hard as he can, my darling. He will be so surprised at how pretty you are, and how handsome your brother is."

Bo just smiled at his sister. He was having a real hard time believing in his dad. It had been a hard thing to watch him get so wasted and neglect them.

He remembered coming home from school one day, calling out for his mom, but she was gone. He realized his dad was downstairs with someone.

He went to the stairway and called out, but they didn't seem to hear him. He went down the hall to see if his baby sister was okay. She was just lying there staring at the ceiling, not even crying.

He got her out of the crib by himself and toted her into the living room to put her in her carrier. He went to the basement steps again and called real loud, "Dad?"

Jimmy stumbled up the stairs and said, "What, buddy? What do you need?"

"Nothing, I just wanted to see if you need me to play with Sky for a while. I think she's wet, Dad."

"Go get a diaper, Buddy; I'll get a bottle warmed up."

There was a lady standing by his dad when he came back. Bo didn't know her and just stared. She was pretty and had real long hair. She said, "Hi there, little fellow. How are you?"

"Fine. Who are you?" Bo was staring at her, wondering why she was here.

Jimmy said, "Bo, this is our neighbor, Chris. Now go on and start your homework, Son." Bo had looked in on Skyler once more, tickling her a little to make her laugh. He headed to his room, plunking down on his bed.

That was about all Bo remembered because soon after that day, his dad got sent to jail for drugs. He heard his mom talking, and she said the lady next door was a *snitch*. Bo didn't know what that meant then…later he would figure it out.

Rose said, "We're stopping for gas kids. If you want something, or if you need to go to the bathroom, please do so now. I'm not sure when you will get another chance."

The kids trekked into the station for snacks and were pretty silent as they buckled back up for the remainder of the drive. Rose was thoughtful as well and turned the radio up, letting the soft rock waft through the silence. She wasn't hearing the music though; she was very diligently saying prayers in her mind that Jimmy would not disappoint them.

She was hopeful for the guy. She knew he had a troubled childhood, getting arrested for burglary at such a young age, but Jimmy was not a bad guy. She was willing to allow him to prove himself a good father. The kids needed a father and it was for them, that she was doing this.

She got to the exit and stopped to consult the directions. They still had to go five miles down Main Street before she would reach the road he was waiting on. Jimmy told her the Jack in the Box was at the second light. She entered the drive through and ordered lunch for all four of them.

As Rose drew closer to the destination, she was tossing the situation around in her head. She still had legal custody of the kids. Bo wouldn't turn eighteen for two more years. She needed to make sure Jimmy knew that she would have to be consulted before the kids could go anywhere with him, or even have a visit.

Her worst fear was that he would try to take them from her somehow, and revisit his drug abuse and neglectful ways. She could never allow that to happen, and just the thought of it twisted something around in her gut. The worry was there on her face, but she never let them see it.

Jimmy was pacing back and forth in front of the window of the halfway house. It was laden with smudges from the faces that had previously peered out, watching and waiting. Mostly grown men, but some half boy, they had all looked out this window through the years…waiting for their stilted lives to start again.

The sills were studied, as the clock ticked and tiny flecks from paint that had been applied decades ago was examined and toyed with. The curtains were old and not even worth the Goodwill bin. They served a purpose of hanging there and that was all.

No one cared to wash, paint or care for this place. It was just a temporary shelter in the interim of someplace that held warmth. There would be a place for him that was warm again, he vowed, a place that he could truly rest his head.

He was happy to be out of the joint, but this dump was cold and drafty. He was determined to stay out and stay clean.

"Where is that old hag?" he thought to himself. He was pondering on all of the anxiety of seeing the kids again. He wondered how they felt about him.

He was grateful for Rose on one hand, but in his mind, she stood between him and his kids. She had power and prestige, and she made Jimmy feel like something that was stuck on the bottom of her shoe. He resented the fact that she had full custody and all of the rights to the kids. Hell, if he wanted to take them to 6-Flags he would have to ask her permission.

The black Mercedes slowly crawled past the brownstone. He thought to himself that she was going to go right on past and she did, but then he saw the tail lights and was about to jump right out of his skin when they backed up and pulled into the driveway.

It was a bad neighborhood. The city of Belleville was filled with pockets of very well maintained large brick homes, but this was not one of them. The place where Jimmy was to spend the next six months was in shambles. The city bought it and renovated it to be barely livable. There were cheap countertops and cupboards. Even cheaper flooring led up to the entryway. It was wide open now, to reveal a ratty and rusting screen door. The house was over sixty years old, and it smelled like it. The musty odor was caused from mildewing wood, and wet wallpaper. Years of leaky faucets and deteriorating window frames, allowed mold to grow behind the drywall.

Jimmy leaned the screen door open and waved, then he popped his head back in and took a big gulp of air to steady his nerves. *They had come. They were here.*

He grabbed a bag from the hall table and went on out.

The doors were slowly opening, and Jimmy watched and held his breath as his kids came into view for the first time in eight years.

Rose came toward him, holding out her hand. "Hello, Jimmy."

"Hi, Rose. You're looking well."

She turned and waved the kids over. They seemed petrified to move any closer, so Jimmy took a step toward them. Rose suddenly put her arm out to block him from proceeding forward.

She said very softly, "Go slow, they do not know you anymore, Jimmy." He paled, but nodded, and stood still waiting for the kids to come over to him.

Bo put his arm around Sky and said, "Come on, let's go check out our dad." She looked up at her brother, wanting to see if he was afraid, but Bo just smiled and nodded to her.

He said, "I don't think he'll bite."

It felt funny to look at him. He was real skinny and short. Bo remembered him being taller, with a beer gut. Eight years had definitely taken its toll. He looked about forty-five, but Bo knew his dad was only thirty-six.

"Hi, kids," he said, they both looked at him and said, "Hi."

"Wow, I can't believe you're really here… Bo, you're a chip off of the old block. I had no idea you would get so tall. And Sky, aw, pumpkin, look at the beautiful little girl you are." He started to shake his head back and forth just staring at them.

"I don't suppose you remember me very well, Bo, it sure has been a long time. Thank you so much for coming to visit." Jimmy felt like he was going to bust out crying, but he shook it off.

He said, "I have a few presents for you guys. Bo, I've been collecting coins for a few years now, and I want you to have them. Have you ever collected coins before?"

Bo shook his head and took the bag that was handed out to him.

"Thanks, Dad," he said. "I haven't ever really checked out a coin collection. Wow, they look really awesome." He gave his dad an awkward grin at receiving the gift.

"You are most welcome, Son." He held out his hand and Bo shook it.

Jimmy knelt down on his knees and gestured Sky to come over to him. When she did, and he saw her face, he felt his breath hitch. She was like an angel in heaven and Jimmy felt himself weeping as he gazed into her crystal blue eyes. He swiped at a tear, he was losing it.

"Sorry, wow, you're just so pretty," he said to her. "I have something very special for you, my sweet, a bracelet and necklace that I made for you." He handed her a thin silver bangle with a tiny heart charm floating on it, and a necklace on a thin chain to match.

Sky smiled at him and said, "Thank you. They're really nice. Thanks."

"Oh Sky, I'm so sorry, baby. I was such a fool to get involved in the stuff I did. I can never make it up to you guys for the time I've been gone, but I swear I'm going to be a good dad to you from here on out, okay? No more trouble, I'm going to do right by you two!" As he made this declaration, still on his knees, the kids remained still. They never stepped farther than an arms reach of their grandmother.

Jimmy's eyes continued to water up. He swiped at his nose and spoke.

"Thank you, Rose." He stood, took a step toward her, and continued. "I can never repay you for bringing them here and letting me see my babies. I'm real sorry for being a jerk. I hope you can find it in your heart to forgive me."

Rose looked him in the eye, "We all make mistakes. The kids and I are glad you're out now. Just remember they have a happy stable home with me, and I'll never allow anything or anyone to mess that up."

She went over to him and put her hand on his shoulder. Then she lowered her voice to an intimate level that only he could hear and said, "Don't ever try and take them, Jimmy. I will fight you with everything I have if you do. Are we clear?"

Jimmy was slightly stunned by her vehemence, but he just nodded his head and told her she would get only gratitude from him. He hadn't forgotten her efforts to bond him out. It was no one's fault but his own that he'd been convicted and sent up the river for eight long years.

Rose gathered the food and they headed over to an outdoor table and chairs. They gingerly sat down after clearing the chairs of bird droppings. They laughed at the cold fries, but all in all, it was a good visit.

Jimmy asked again if they could all forgive him and return soon for another visit.

Rose got quiet for a minute, and then she told him that it was time to show some character. She grabbed his hand, nodded to the kids and said, "We will pray." They dutifully bowed their heads and Jimmy did as well.

She started, "Heavenly Father, we ask that you continue to work in Jimmy's heart to heal any sickness that is still living in his spirit. Restore him Lord.... to the man that is clean and white and let him see the blessings that are here in his presence today. Lord we ask you in Jesus' name. Amen."

The kids said "Amen," and heard a small "Amen," come from their father. Then they all opened their eyes and smiled. Rose was hopeful, but she needed to reiterate one more time that legally she was the only one that held parental custody.

She looked Jimmy square in the eye and told him if he slipped up, they would not be back. She held her hand out to him and he shook it. They headed over to the car and the kids hugged Jimmy good-bye.

The visit had gone well, and Rose was relieved. She put the car in reverse and left the Belleville halfway house and her grandchildren's father, the convict, behind her.

On the ride home, she asked the kids how they felt it went. Both of them had been watching her. They needed to know if she approved of their father.

She told them it was important for them to remember he was only human. All men on Earth are full of sin and human frailties and we are all deserving of God's love because we are His children. She assured the kids of her confidence in Jimmy. She felt he was going to try and be there for them from now on, but if that did not happen, she would take care of them.

The meeting she'd dreaded for years was over, and now, Rose was just ready to don her slippers and sit out on the veranda with some citrus tea. She needed to brace herself for the fact that soon, Jimmy would be able to travel around and ask to take the kids here and there. She was not ready for that, but it was not always going to be just a matter of her saying "yes" or "no." She would have to take into consideration that Jimmy loved the kids and her hope was that he could love himself just as much.

Ninety-two miles away, Jimmy was sitting at the old table smoking a Marlboro red. He was all confused with his feelings. The old hag had been good to bring the kids today. God, they were amazing. Bo looked just like him when he was sixteen, and Sky was so pretty, just like Annie. He wondered about Annie a lot through the years. There was a smattering of letters in that first year, but after that, it was like she dropped off of the face of the Earth.

He wanted to see her again. He wanted to ask her why she'd run off and left the kids with Rose…(not that he wasn't glad). He knew in his gut Annie wasn't strong enough to take care of the kids without him. She'd never handled motherhood well. He was the one that washed clothes and changed diapers, while Annie was doing her nails and coloring her long blonde hair.

The truth was they were both losers. Rose knew it and God bless her; she was good enough not to keep the kids from him. That was something he felt real grateful for.

He needed them. He wanted to try and be somebody that was worthy of being a father. It was all he thought about as he sat in jail, doing right by his kids.

Maybe Rose would let him come and try to settle close by. He would show her he could do it all. He'd get a job, make a life, and stay clean. He wanted to teach Bo to drive, and he wanted Sky to call him *Daddy*.

⇒ 4 ⇐
The Gift

It was Sunday. Rose was giving a sermon today, at the Rivers Oak Christian Church. The people all raised their faces to listen, as the woman stepped to the pulpit to spread her message.

She was prepared and she started to talk about what was on her heart this day:

> *"A small boy had broken a lamp with a ball and never told anyone. Upon finding the lamp broken his mother asked him what had happened and he said, "I don't know, I didn't do it." She waited for her husband to come home. The small boy and his brother took their places at the dinner table. Their mother brought up the mysterious broken lamp. As their father asked them for the truth, the smallest boy again*

denied responsibility. His brother looked at him and said, "You are telling a lie." The younger son abruptly left the table and ran upstairs. The father looked at his wife and eldest son and said, "I will go and see to him." He went upstairs, searching everywhere for his son. He was not in the places he would normally be. Upon entering the master bedroom, the child was finally located. He was in the center of the bed huddled there deeply, amongst the covers. His father said, "Come here, Son." The boy let out a barely audible, "No" and he huddled there, digging deeper in his shame. He was sweating and hot, barely able to breath, and he was hiding his face. Finally his father crawled up and gently pulled the covers off of his youngest son. He told him, "Son, don't you know that whatever you do…I could never love you any less?" The boy went to his father and held onto him sobbing, "I'm Sorry, Dad." His father said, "I know Son, I forgive you…and remember, that God loves all of us just like that. No matter what we do, He will never love us any less."

Rose was talking now, about how we all fall short of the grace of God. This was a sermon she loved, "The errant little boy." It's a reminder that we are loved unconditionally.

In her unconscious mind somewhere, she was struggling to remember the message in reference to Jimmy and Annie. They had let her and the kids down, but she knew that forgiveness was not only an option, but also a necessity. It was just a given.

Two months had passed by, and Jimmy called the house asking if he could see the kids again. Rose told him that he had to wait until spring break, which was in a few more weeks. She made plans to free her schedule and do some special outings with the kids. She was looking forward to taking them to dinner and maybe to the Science Center or the Art Museum. She was thinking they could schedule in a visit with their father as well.

It was going to be a pizza party this time. They were bringing school photos and some other pictures from events of the past eight years.

As the day arrived, the mood was lighter. The kids were completely relaxed as they thought about the man that waited to see them. They piled into the vehicle and set out for Belleville. As hills turned to fields of green pasture and hay bales, they commented on the cows grazing. They chattered on about Rose's 58th birthday, and how they wanted to have a party for her. The sun was shining and they were enjoying the company of one another.

They were an hour into the trip, when Sky, who had been lightly napping in the back, let out a scream. She sat up and grabbed Rose's shoulder and said, "Grandma, get off the highway now!"

Rose just looked at her and frowned. "Whatever in the world are you going on about Skyler?" she asked her granddaughter, who was now growing frantic with her request that they take the next exit.

Rose turned on her blinker, exited the highway and pulled over to the shoulder. She turned her head to look at Sky. "Well?" she asked, and Sky just kept looking behind them at the freeway they had just exited.

Then suddenly, without warning there were sirens and within three seconds, screaming squad cars were flying by with lights blazing. The air was rent with fire trucks on the horns, and brakes squealing as traffic took to the shoulder to escape the melee.

Rose felt her throat tighten. She turned in her seat and looked at her granddaughter. She asked, "How did you know that we were in the path of that Sky?"

Sky just shrugged her shoulders and said, "I had my eyes closed, and I saw what was coming at us. I knew that we could've gotten killed Grandma. It's been happening to me every once in a while, and I don't know why."

Rose slowly turned back around in her seat and said to herself, "Dear Lord, what kind of special gift have you given this child?" She was in shock, and as they proceeded to gain the highway again, she kept looking at the kids in the rearview mirror.

Bo said, "You know, Sky, you have tried to tell me when to stay home and when to go places. Did you see things the night Billy and I went to the skate rink, and that kid got taken? You didn't want me to go that night."

She was thoughtful for a second. "I saw something dark happening in that place sometime that night. I wasn't sure what, where, or who it would involve. First, I woke up to a bright light, then, I saw a foggy picture and your face."

"You told me that you were not having a good feeling about that place, I remember. Is this what you meant, Skyler? That you saw something happening?" She nodded at Bo.

"I didn't see the boy being taken. I didn't know someone was going to be abducted. It doesn't make any sense I know. But, a shadow of a man was near you."

Rose said, "We need to find someone to talk to tomorrow and see what we can learn about these visions. I'm really in shock right now. I don't understand this kind of thing."

Sky said, "I don't understand it either and I don't want to see these things, Grandma."

"Don't worry, it's going to be okay." Rose continued driving, while talking to her softly, reassuring her they would find out what was happening.

The visit with Jimmy went smoothly. He talked about his roomies at the halfway house, and their stories. He told the kids that more than ever he needed them to know he was going to rehabilitate himself, and get a place of his own as soon as possible.

They listened, hopeful that what he was telling them would happen. All the while their minds were on what they had just discovered about Skyler.

Rose gathered her up after school the following Monday, and took her to a building that housed the office of a very unique man. His name was Matthew Roads. He had written many articles on the "Mysteries of the Mind," and had come to see her speak a few times. He was a Christian, a psychiatrist and an author.

Matthew was sitting in a great leather chair as they entered. He stood and came over to the door to usher them in. He waved them over to the couch, and told them to get comfortable. He asked if they would like water, as he gestured to the water cooler and paper cups in the corner by the window.

As they both declined, Rose introduced her granddaughter. Matthew shook her hand, and studied the ten year old. He noticed the peculiar lightness in her eyes. Her pupils were surrounded by a distinct shade of light blue. It was uncommon to be sure. The shade was so rare that it reminded him of an icy blue mountain. It struck him that he'd never gazed into eyes such as hers.

He stood by the desk a moment in thought, before gathering up his pad and pen. He wrote the date and time, and went around to sit at his desk.

He began the consultation by switching on a small tape recorder. He made a formal request before beginning.

"Do I have both of your permission to record our conversation today?" he asked them. They both answered, "*Yes*" so he started his inquisition. "Rose, I am going to ask you to speak first. Can you briefly summarize what has happened with Skyler?"

Rose told him what had happened the Saturday before, and he wrote something down on his ledger.

"Skyler, how old were you, if you can recall for me, the first time you felt like you knew something was going to happen?" he asked.

She began to tell him; "I was about four, I think, when I woke up feeling like I was seeing something that was going to happen. It was almost always with Bo, or our dogs.

"One of the scariest times happened when I was at the pool napping in the sun, and Matilda was barking at the woods. As I was lying there, all of the sudden I had a vision of something storming out and attacking her. I was so scared, I grabbed her up and ran as fast as I could up to my room and locked the door." She scrunched up her shoulders and shook her head, "I was just so scared of the vision I had, because it was so violent. I was six then."

Rose rubbed her shoulder, telling her to close her eyes and just relax. "It's okay, Honey, just tell Dr. Roads what happened. Take your time."

Sky took a breath and then proceeded to tell them what happened next that confirmed her vision. She said, "The next day after he got off the bus, Bo ran into the house screaming that he'd seen a coyote at the property line. It was frantically digging. He felt like it had found it's way into the compound under a fence and it was confused as to how to escape. Grandma called the animal control people and it was very viscous and stood growling at them. They relocated it out of city limits near a preservation forest. It was a good thing it had not attacked anyone or anything on the property as it got closer seeking food and escape.

"I never told anyone about it," she continued. "I had some kind of intuition and I thought maybe it was normal and that everyone had it."

"Well," Matthew told her, "In a lot of cases we do have intuition, but it is rare that one can sense a violent episode before it begins."

Sky told him that there was another time she had experienced a horrifying vision. She was seven. He asked her to please explain it to them as best she could and to take her time.

She looked over at her grandmother and began the tale. Rose sat enthralled by what she was hearing Sky say. Her ten-year-old voice was clear and sweet as she recited the scary vision.

"It was winter, and it was icy out. Grandma was coming back from an engagement in Atlanta. Her flight was to arrive in the morning at 8 AM. I knew that because she always wrote everything down for us on the refrigerator. We always had a phone number for emergencies and we always had her schedule. If we needed to reach her, she always wanted to make sure we could." She smiled at Rose, and continued with her statements.

"It was around midnight, when I suddenly woke up. I heard a roaring in my ears. I was groggy and I knew I had been dreaming, but was now awake. I shook my head trying to clear it, but it was right there in front of me, happening so vividly. It was horrible. I was seeing a great fire up in the mountains! There was a roaring coming from the fire and the smoke filled my nose and burned my eyes. There was a wing of an airplane sticking up and I heard screaming. That's when I realized that I was seeing something that was going to happen. I'm not sure how I knew, but I felt instinctually it was my grandma's airplane. I felt terrified, so I went to the kitchen to get the number to call her."

"Grandma answered right away. She was sleeping. I told her I had dreamed of an airplane crash, and I asked her to please fly later. She just poo pooed my concerns and told me to get some warm milk and go back to bed...but, I couldn't. I sat and stared at the clock for hours, then called her again at 5 AM. "She told me to, stop it. She said everything was fine and she would be home soon. I was so scared; I went up to my room and cried for an hour straight. Remember Grandma?"

Rose had tears streaming out of her eyes now. She was in disbelief that Skyler had actually seen the crash. She nodded, and stayed quiet, letting the story continue.

Sky was looking at Matthew now. "At about 6:30 that morning, I was outside letting Martin and Matilda go potty, when I heard the phone ringing inside. I ran to answer it. Grandma was explaining, she had missed her flight because of traffic. There was nothing to be done a bad wreck had closed off the only artery leading to the airport, so she would not make the flight. I was elated and went back up to my room to lie down. I finally slept."

Sky stopped and requested a small cup of that water now. She sipped a moment, and continued.

"Then, at about 10:30 or so, I was sitting at the breakfast bar eating a bowl of cereal, watching TV when the station broke in with a news bulletin: an Atlantic Flight #247 had crashed in the Smokey Mountains. There were no known survivors. The flight was destined for St. Louis, Missouri. I remember being shocked as I sat there watching the news footage. My stomach was queasy, as I saw the smoke and the wing again. It was exactly like my vision. That's when I knew I had really seen something bad. I got upset."

"Grandma came in around noon that day and I ran to her and hugged her so tight. I couldn't explain or begin to understand, so I just didn't bring it up." Skyler had been looking down at her hands and fidgeting with her nails, but now she looked at both of them in turn.

"Do you remember that, Grandma?" she asked Rose.

Rose sat there stunned. She had no idea, no clue that all of that was going on in Skyler's mind back then. She remembered the crash though, but she'd just thought it was a coincidence that Skyler had dreamed of a plane crash.

"I'm sorry, Matthew, it's just that I have a hard time believing in this kind of phenomenon. I am deeply concerned for Skyler." She continued to fuss a moment and he offered her a box of Kleenex.

Sky reached over and hugged her grandmother. She said, "I'm sorry, Grandma I'm not sure what's happening, but there's a lot more. Are you going to be all right? Do you think we should take a break?"

Rose was just beside herself with worry and confusion. She looked at Matthew and asked him a question, "Have you ever encountered this before?"

He told her it was highly uncommon, but there were definitely documented cases where individuals had a gift of "sight" which is what they called it here in the world of psychic phenomena. He felt all cases were unique, including Skyler's.

"We have a few case files that I will bring to our next consultation to share with you. We can correlate some of the details and see if we can find any common denominators."

Rose stood up and told him that she would be in touch. He urged her to write down anything and everything Sky says she sees.

"It will take time," he explained. "We need to set up a complete physical and mental evaluation at the first opportunity." He asked them both if that was okay.

Sky nodded her head and said, "I'm kind of shocked myself, but I can't help what I see when I close my eyes. I'm scared. I want to be normal. I don't want to have these visions. It's really freaking me out."

When they got home, Bo was waiting for them and wanted to know what was said. Rose told him, "It is all going to be studied and figured out, but somehow Sky has received something a little special from God. Apparently, she's been given some kind of psychic warning system of doom. It's not going to be easy to grasp, but sometimes these things are just a mystery."

Bo went over to his baby sister and said, "Are you okay?"

She nodded at him, and went in for a bear hug. She said, "Bo, this is just so weird. I never wanted to see bad stuff, but I do. I don't like this feeling. Why do I have to see scary stuff?" She started crying.

Bo held his sister just like when she was a baby. He rocked her and consoled her saying; "It's going to be alright. Don't cry now, grandma and I are here for you."

Skyler slept well for several months, with nothing disturbing her sweet dreams. The household began to return to normal. Matthew warned them to keep pen and paper nearby. Everything was to be recorded immediately, while the details of the vision were clear.

5

Annie Comes Home

Annie England was taking the stage any minute. It was not supposed to be her turn she usually followed Dallas, but Dallas was sick tonight, so Annie was going third.

There was a row out there that she'd been warned about from Eve and Scarlet, the two performers before her. It was the rough crew that came in from the strip joint on the East side of town, called Raunchy Roy's. There were continuous allegations of rough treatment during lap dances and disrespecting all occupants of the Pink Cabaret.

They paid their dancers a pittance compared to what Annie commanded, and it was not the kind of audience she wanted to dance for this evening. *Dang it, she didn't feel like being nice to these freaks!*

She donned her lace shawl, with nothing but a white, sheer, sequined two-piece number underneath. It was designed to show everything she had to show. Black heels and a black Derby completed the skimpy ensemble. She raised her chin at the image she saw in the mirror…gave herself a nod, and proceeded to take the stage.

"Ladies and Gentlemen," the DJ announced, "Here tonight to grace our stage is Lady G. Give her a hand now, folks."

The tune by Joe Cocker started to gently play, rising in volume. Suddenly the music took a quick breath, and she appeared. As the song grew in intensity, she sashayed, waltzed and swayed to, *You Can Leave Your Hat On*."

Annie had been dancing now for several years. She was good and the squalor in the back row decided they wanted the first row. They moved forward as if in a chess game, one guy shoving another guy, and making him give up his seat.

As they advanced closer to Annie, she felt a sudden premonition as she looked at the one directly in front of her. He was tensing his fist over and over, and there was a glazed look on his face as he leered at her.

One thing was for sure; she needed to have security watch over this one tonight. He was giving off a real foul odor as well. She smelled sweat and garlic. That was something Annie was not on board with, a dirty man touching her. She wondered if her boyfriend Ivan would come in a little early tonight.

She enjoyed the stage, but the club had grown seedy and disgusting in the light of day. She wanted to get as far away from it as possible, after she performed her job for the audience.

Meanwhile, she gestured to Rob, the bouncer, with her hand on her head, shaking it. That was a sign that he needed to move in closer, and be alert to rabble-rousers. When a man got drunk and belligerent, there were a few ways to quickly remove him from the establishment, and Rob specialized in both. They were designed to render him unable to swing or walk. At that time the offender would be dragged or lifted toward the door.

It was almost time for the next number. She was finishing up her gyrations at the end with only the G-string and the hat on, when the big goon in the front suddenly got up and grabbed her.

Rob got on his back and tried to get him into a wrestling hold. The goon lost his grip, and Annie was brought down off of the stage and slammed to the floor, unconscious.

There was mass pandemonium as the goon hit Rob several times, and grabbed Annie, picking her up and running out the door with her. It had all happened fast. The crowd was surging forward and fleeing all at once, creating a tornado of twisting and turning swarms that blocked the path of Rob, as he tried to pursue Annie's kidnapper.

The black SUV jumped the curb, howled out of the parking lot and headed down the highway before any one could stop it. It was mid-night.

Eighty-five miles away, Skyler woke up and saw something that made her scream out. She flew down the hall and into her grandmothers' room. She was acting frenzied and desperate in her insistence.

"Grandma, Grandma, they're taking her to the river. Hurry, somebody stop them. They're going to kill her and throw her in the river!"

Rose was barely awake, but all of a sudden she got completely alert and said, "Who Sky? Who are you seeing, Honey?" and Sky looked at her with those huge blue eyes fringed in black lashes. The tears were streaming down her face and she was almost incoherent.

She said, "It's…my mother."

Rose dialed 9-11, and the police came screaming to the house. Within nine minutes of the call, they were descending on the room where Sky was lying with an ice pack on her eyes, drinking a cup of warm milk.

A total of four officers, stood in front of the little girl. Carla had brought them in and they quieted as they took in the scene. Rose was sitting beside her granddaughter with her hand on Skyler's leg.

She started to answer the questions, but was becoming inconsolable as she told them she'd seen a vision; in it, her mother was being taken to the river. She saw her mother's body being roughly thrown in.

"Somebody please do something!" She cried, "She doesn't have much time."

Rose told them about Annie, and that she was a dancer at the Pink Cabaret. It was where she probably was, or had last been. The police were making calls, and within five minutes they had processed the fact that a call had just been answered. It was confirmed that indeed Annie England had been taken out of the club and transported north in a black Lincoln Navigator.

They put out an immediate APB on the vehicle, but no one had gotten the plates. They did have a man in custody at the City of East St. Louis Police Dept. He was seen on video entering the establishment with the suspects and was being questioned at this time.

Skyler was beside herself. She'd seen a violent act, but she also knew that it could be averted if they could get to her mother.

It was dark in the old building. Annie was trying shake off the dizziness. They'd tied her up and were in the process of trying to transport her to a very important client that had pointed Annie out as *the one* he wanted. She was trying real hard to focus. She was freezing in the warehouse. They had not given her any clothes.

Big John or "bone crusher" as they called him, came in and told her that if she made any trouble, it was going to be lights out. They were sending Annie to Chicago, but first she had to get a dose of a very powerful sedative. They came over to her and the big guy held her down, while the other goon that had taken her put his arm on her neck.

He growled at her, "You better not move or fight me, because I can smash your windpipe and break your pretty neck without any effort at all, *kabeesh?*"

He untied her and was checking her arms. He started to attempt putting a tourniquet on her arm. He brought over a black bag and opened it. There was an assembly of hypodermic supplies in the bag and he picked up a few articles and closed it. He unwrapped a tiny, square shaped foil packet. His fingers were big and clumsy and he dropped it, cussing.

This is the moment she chose to fight. One thing about Annie was she could be a spitfire. If she decided she was not going to do something, it would be a hell of a fight to make her.

Big John punched her in the jaw, trying not to mark her face up, but he wasn't having a good time trying to get this one to go down. She got still for a moment, and then all of a sudden she kicked out which startled him. He staggered backward. She went at him and punched him straight in the neck. He was taken by surprise and Annie got up and started running.

Another thing about Annie was she ran like a gazelle. Her long legs were thrashing and kicking her way through that place. She was hysterical, but she could see a huge EXIT sign, and she was hell bent on reaching it before the big goons could catch her. She hit the door hard, it gave, and she flew out of there like the hounds of hell were on her tail.

Two squad cars were cruising Water Street, when they spotted her running. They screamed toward her and saw two men were pursuing her.

Officer Kenny Nolan was the first one to intercede the scantily clad woman. He grabbed her and put her on the ground and told her to stay there…then he aimed his firearm at Big John and said, "Cease, lie down on the ground! You're under arrest!"

His partner had subdued another nasty goon. Within minutes, both men were being held down in the middle of the dark river front road at gunpoint.

More officers were gathering at the scene. Annie was put into an ambulance and covered by several blankets. She was in shock, but her vitals were good. They rushed her off to the hospital for further observation.

Her face was swollen from crying, her jaw was bruised, and she was shaken very badly. It had been the scariest thing that ever happened to her. She told them she'd barely escaped. In two more seconds she would have been shot up with drugs and transported to Chicago.

The police told her the two goons had been identified. They were involved in a human trafficking ring. They had been under surveillance for several months.

They were en route to the hospital. Officer Nolan was gently questioning Annie England. He was writing it all down, documenting time and the condition of the rescued woman.

When the call came in that Annie was in an emergency vehicle, on its way to the hospital, Rose was brought to her knees. She thanked God that her only child was safe.

Annie was amazed at her good fortune to be rescued; she felt it was a miracle. She was telling them thank you. That's when they told her about the call from her mother alerting the police that she was in trouble. Annie pondered on this a second.

"Wait, how did she know anything was wrong? I don't understand." She sat on the gurney trembling, looking at the police for answers. Officer Nolan explained.

"We were alerted about an abduction that had taken place, and that a woman was being taken towards the river. The call came in shortly after 12:10 AM. We were patrolling the riverfront when you appeared."

Annie was completely confused but entirely grateful. She was feeling shaky while they processed her into the hospital room and got her into a bed. She was given a complete examination. The doctor told her he was giving her fluids and keeping her for a few hours to stabilize her, but she would be fine, and asked her if there was someone she needed to call.

She remembered Ivan, but had no phone with her. She asked to use the phone and Officer Nolan brought it to her. First, she called Ivan. He told her he would be right there. Then she called her mother.

"Mom?" she said, "How did you know to call the police?" Rose had no idea where to begin the explanation, but she tried.

"It was Skyler, Annie. She saw everything in a dream and woke up to tell me you were going to be thrown in the river. She's right here, hold on." Rose decided to just let Sky tell her.

Sky, who had been lying on the couch, sprang up completely on alert when the phone rang, and was now beside Rose.

"Skyler honey, your mom wants to ask you some questions." Rose handed the phone to Sky, nodding her head in encouragement. On the other end, Annie was gently crying.

"I'm not sure what has happened here, but thank you for telling Grandma what you saw. What did you see, Sweetheart?"

"I woke up with a vision in my head of you and two bad men. It was so real and I knew what was going to happen. They were so mean and violent. One of them was real big and he was going to kill you. I had to get someone to listen, because I knew you didn't have much time."

Annie, on the other end with blankets wrapped around her, was sobbing.

"I'm so confused Skyler. I don't understand what you're saying to me." Sky reiterated again, that she just woke up with a vision. All she knew was that her Mom was going to be thrown into the river. She told Annie that she was not sure why she saw stuff, but that it was starting to happen more frequently. The visions were scary and they frightened her.

"I'll be home in a few days, Skyler. We need to sit down and talk, okay?"

"Okay Mom, I'm glad you are safe now. I love you."

"I love you too, Pumpkin. I'll see you soon." Annie hung up and pondered on what had just been said to her. It was too much to comprehend.

Ivan came and took Annie back to her place in the city. He was watching her, thinking about the fact that she was changed somehow. She wasn't responding to him, he figured she was in shock and needed some time to heal.

The abduction from the club and what had almost happened to her had changed Annie. She was focusing today, seeing things clearly, and becoming aware of how dangerous her life was. She had taken her safety, and her health for granted, going day to day in some kind of fog. She lived in a lethargic state, not really living at all, as she slept all day, spending each night in a club full of strangers.

She pulled out her wallet and brought out pictures of Skyler and Bo. A tear slipped down her face as she thought of the last time she saw them. She had gotten into her car and driven away without a second glance. Her thoughts had been on practicing her new routine. She was anxious to try on outfits that would make her stand out. It was all shallow, never heartfelt as she did what she thought was making her happy. She'd been a shitty mother. She needed to try and find some redemption. She had come very close to death and somehow it made her want more from life.

It was a gorgeous day. Skyler sat waiting for her mother. She was rocking Matilda back and forth in the old swing up on the porch, wondering about what she was going to tell her mom. It was all so strange and the visions were unexplainable really. She was some kind of freak, she supposed.

Annie had not visited her mother's home in several years. Once a summer she tried to see the kids, but the years had blended into one another. It had been two since she had come here, to the compound. Now, there was something happening to her child, and although they were weak, the maternal instincts were kicking in. She needed to make sure Sky was okay.

She pulled into the long driveway in her red Ford Fusion, and saw Sky sitting on the porch. She parked and got out, heading up the walk. As she perused the familiar landscaping, it occurred to her that the trees had gotten taller, and the bushes thicker around the grounds. She looked at the upstairs window where her mother's face stared back at her. She nodded up at Rose, and smiled.

Annie England was not ordinary to look at. Her face was one you could imagine on a magazine cover. She was a cool blonde that exuded charisma. She flowed as she walked with the air of Grace Kelly toward the house. Her clothes were flashy and fun most of the time. Even now, her jean pockets were lined with rhinestones.

There was nothing playful in her mood today. Bruised and aching, Annie had a stone cold sober look on her face, as she sought out the gaze of her little girl up on the porch.

Home was never an easy place for her. She felt the need to search for something she would never find here…within the fenced compound. It was illusive, and had wings that lifted her up, giving her the excitement of an endless roller coaster ride.

Annie was of the "*Free bird*" era, and sang it loud along with Leonard Skynard as it blared from her speakers. "*Lord, I can't chay ange…won't cha buy uy free bird yeaaa*" Now, she stood in front of her daughter.

"Hi, Muffin, I guess it's time we had a chat. Let's take a walk. I would love to go down to the lake and sit in the gazebo, how about you?" She reached out her hand.

Sky nodded and taking her mothers hand, they started down the walk.

Rose sat watching them through the window. She had not seen Annie for two years, and it was good to lay eyes on her only child. A tear slipped down her face as she remembered with poignancy the scene she was watching. Her memory of holding Annie's hand was vivid.

She reminisced a moment, remembering her little girl skipping and laughing as they walked down the well-worn path. Time had given Rose a mirror, and as she looked at her daughter, she saw herself. She was grateful Annie was here.

The two gathered up pinecones as they walked, chatting about nothing in particular. Annie asked Sky if she had a boyfriend.

"No, boys are dumb. They act eight, instead of ten." Annie laughed out loud.

"I think I was 14 before I actually realized they were fascinating creatures, so you have time." She was laughing and Skyler laughed back.

They were seated in the old gazebo, looking up at a bird's nest in the corner of the structure, when Annie asked Sky to talk to her about the visions. Skyler was scraping at the paint on the arm of the bench, trying to find the words she wanted.

"It's kind of scary because I never know when it's going to wake me up. At first it's a really bright light, then foggy images start coming to me. My stomach feels shaky, and I get real anxious to get help. The counselor says it's very rare to have the ability to predict events." She looked at her mom asking, "Have you ever heard of this before, Mom?"

Annie was completely at a loss for words that would offer the comfort Sky was seeking from her.

"I'm sorry, Muffin, but I don't know anyone that has this kind of gift. I'll bet Grandma can find out things though, because she knows so many people around the world. There has to be other cases like this. What did you see exactly, when I was taken?" she asked.

"Well," Sky began, "A man had you and was carrying you on his back. You were lifeless, like a rag doll. He was going toward the river and he was going to throw you in. There was another man even bigger following and yelling at the one that had you. He was saying, *"If we get out of this one, I'm clearing out of here. You really screwed it up now, Lou!"* She closed her eyes a moment, remembering and describing the scene.

"The water was making a noise and it was rushing under a bridge. There was a bad smell of dead fish and rotten garbage. You were barely breathing." Sky looked up at her mom then, feeling emotional. She continued her description.

"When I saw your face, it was almost blue and I woke up. I ran and told Grandma and she called the police. It's not the first time I have seen things, Mom. I'm not sure when it will happen again, but it's scaring me."

"You saved my life, Sky." Annie was reaching toward her to embrace her. A rare time and as Annie gazed into her little girls bright vivid blue gaze, she knew she needed to stay close. There was something energetic happening as they hugged. It was as if a spark was traveling through them and if the light were doused, they would be lit up from some inner source.

Sky was reveling in her mothers scent. She realized that she and her mom were forming a bond. This was one of the best days of her life. She was thinking the vision had happened to bring them together. Maybe it was a good thing, because it probably helped to save her mother's life.

That evening, Annie, Sky, Rose, and Bo ate dinner together. They talked about seeing Jimmy and prayed for him to stay straight. He would be free very soon now, and there was anxiety about him being around the kids.

Annie asked if he knew about Skyler's gift of sight, and they told her *no,* they were not going to tell anyone about it. Rose was adamant that Sky was to lead a normal life and do what she always does: go to school and have activities and friends. The last thing she wanted was for anyone to try and interview Skyler.

The thought of the public and the paparazzi trying to storm the compound was a disturbing one for Rose. She guarded the privacy of her home like nothing else. She made a mental note to alert Ben, her head of security, to do a check on the exterior of the property. She needed to make sure the cameras were all working and the motion detectors were functioning as well. The fortress she had built around herself was going to be challenged, if any of this information about Skyler was leaked to the press.

The next morning Rose went down to get the paper. There was a story about Annie's attempted abduction, but it was brief. They talked about breaking up a human trafficking ring, and that a dancer was found safe. Her name was used, but Rose didn't think it would lead to any follow-up stories. For now, they were in the clear, and Annie was content to be home for a few days.

Lunch was being served outside on the patio. Bo and Carla joined the others.

"You need to eat Ms. Annie. Let Carla make you a big burrito. I put beans, cheese and sour cream on it for you, si?"

"Gracias, Carla, I would love that."

"We will make you strong again, Nina, you'll see."

Annie was enjoying the pampering. She hardly took her eyes off of the kids. They had changed so much these last few years. The babyhood was long gone, never to return. She barely remembered those days, of rocking and tickling. It hit her abruptly that she had missed out on them altogether. She wasn't very proud of herself for that.

Bo was talking to her, saying he had a job now. She smiled at him. He was handsome and sweet; she wanted to have a chance to know him. Maybe it wasn't too late; maybe she was right where she needed to be.

Carla set the big burrito before her and said, "Eat."

Annie laughed, "Yes ma'am…it looks amazing."

Rose said, "I'll say a blessing."

> "Heavenly Father, We thank you for this lovely day and this lovely meal. Thank you for bringing Annie home safe, Lord. I know you are watching over all of us…keeping us safe. Thank you Father. Thank you Jesus. Amen"

They all said, "Amen" and then there was no sound, except the appreciative noises of a delicious meal being shared…and the occasional begging of Martin and Matilda, as they cried for crumbs.

6

Ransom

The day had finally arrived. Jimmy sat waiting for his PO, looking around the elegant office. The room was tastefully decorated with perfectly centered art and a blending of a classic pallet. He was struck with the contrast to the house he had just spent six months living in.

It had taken him over an hour to get here. He rode the metro train, then walked seven blocks. He went to the fourth floor and through a security checkpoint before reaching the office of Manny Fields. This was a very important day.

Manny came in carrying a folder and sat down in the chair across from him. He grinned at Jimmy, and shook his hand. He slapped the folder down on the desk.

"Well, old man, your probation's up, you're free to go. The court stipulates that you check in with me once a month, on the first. Are you okay with that?"

Jimmy was grinning back. He was on cloud nine today. He had tasted freedom again. It was a dish he savored and wanted to keep on his table.

"I'm completely on board with that Manny. I'm anxious to get a job, earn a paycheck and mind my own business. The first thing I need to do though is to start taking care of my kids."

"You got $285.00 that you earned Jimmy. Here's a cashiers check. Can I give you some advice?" Manny sat forward with his hand on his cheek. He always tried to look on the bright side, as he set up the boundaries for parolees to keep their newfound freedom.

Jimmy nodded. Manny leaned toward him and started talking to him in a steely voice.

"Stay sober and stay clean. That's all I'm asking of you Jimmy. The road to jail is through a bottle and a joint. If you want to be right back where you just spent eight years, well then the odds are that you will be. If you value the freedom you now have, you won't touch the substances. Get in the habit of drinking tea and chewing gum. Get a hobby or a project. Draw, write, travel, and enjoy the country. Am I clear?" Jimmy nodded again.

"I got two reasons for living now, Manny. I was addicted before and the drugs were the only thing I was in love with, but now, I got my kids." Manny was smiling at him.

"Yea well, if I had a dollar for every guy that walked in and out of here saying that, I'd be a millionaire. Now go make a life with some chubby woman that can cook and rub your back. Freedom is fragile, Jimmy. Good luck." Jimmy stood up and shook Manny's outstretched hand.

"Thanks Manny, I hope I never see you again." He was laughing as he turned to head out the door. Just as he was about to walk out, Manny said one more thing to him.

"Don't chase money, Jimmy. Chase good, clean decisions, and an honest day's work. Good-bye." Then, he let the door shut on the thirty-sixth man that served his sentence and walked out free this year.

The weekend was coming and Jimmy was making plans to see the kids. He called Rose and asked for a visit. She told him they could meet for dinner and maybe a movie on Saturday. He was great with that and excited. They would confirm the time and place on Saturday morning.

Jimmy was looking for a present for the kids. Sunday was Easter, but they were a little too old for an Easter basket. He didn't have much left from his stash of cash, but he was going to start working at his new job at the Goodwill in Belleville on Monday. Life was looking up; soon he would get a place of his own and start living a normal life.

The following Friday night was a special night. The family reserved this night as much as they could to play games with each other. The kids were playing rummy with Carla, laughing and drinking soda. They were told not to have too much caffeine, as it was getting late. The hours were going by fast and the laughter was interrupted with yawns.

At 9 PM, Rose came in and told them to get into bed, tomorrow they were going out to eat and to the movies with Jimmy. She went into both of their rooms, tucking them in and talking to them about the following day.

Bo lay with his arms up, cradling his neck. He was deeply in thought, and his grandmother asked him how he was feeling.

"It just scares me sometimes. I'm afraid that Dad will go back to being a drug addict. If he has us visit, and I'm not there, I'm afraid he will leave Sky to do drugs or something. I guess I'm more worried that something will happen to her, and I don't want to feel like that, but I don't trust him." Bo was struggling with the insecurities about Jimmy. Rose tried to reassure him.

"I'll keep that in mind, Bo. You know we have to give him a chance. I do need you to talk to me if you have any other concerns from this day forward okay?" She reached over to ruffle his hair and Bo told her, "Okay."

The past eight years had turned Bo from a boy to a bright young man. She felt proud of the way he tended to Sky. In her mind it was a rare bond these two kids had.

Skyler was reading in her room. The book was about a family of fairies and how they built a castle for everyone in the valley to live in. Rose asked her to read some of it to her. As she listened to the clear childish voice, she resolved once again to protect these two cubs from harm.

Sky continued to read aloud and Rose lay down beside her. She said a prayer right then and there in her mind, that no one ever hurt or neglected the kids. She was thinking that God had blessed her in multitude when he brought them here for her to raise. She had never regretted it for a second.

It was sometime in the wee hours of the morning that she heard Sky crying for her.

"Grandma, Grandma!"

Rose got up, and flew down the hall. She sat on the bed and grabbed Skyler up in her arms and held her.

"What is it? What have you seen, child?"

"Two bad men. They're talking about my dad. They have guns and ropes. I can see them talking and they've been watching us. They're following us and I can see a van. It's white and it has one reddish brown door on the side. Oh, Grandma, why am I seeing this? We have to tell someone, because they want to hurt my Dad, or wait, I…I think they want me!"

Rose took a deep breath.

"I'll call the police tomorrow and have them put surveillance on the compound," she reassured Skyler. "We"ll keep you safe I promise, don't worry." But, Rose was worried.

The next day Rose called Jimmy and told him there was something she needed to tell him. They would still meet him, but it would have to be at the mall, where there were lots of people. They were going to eat and see a movie Sunday night..

She called the police department and spoke to an officer about having a patrol car near the gate of the compound. She was told that it was not going to work that way. They were understaffed, and although they would make more frequent rounds, she would have to hire her own hourly security guard.

Rose was so confused as to what she would tell Jimmy. He needed to be told about Skyler's visions. She didn't really think he would believe it. She had no proof really, just the fact that what

Skyler claimed would happen, happened. Annie was going to have to back her up in this.

They were waiting at the mall for him. Jimmy saw his kids sitting on a bench and Rose was looking in a store window. He grinned at them as he walked up.

"Man, it's great to be here. I'm so excited about the movie you guys. How have you two been?" Both kids answered together, "Fine, thanks." Jimmy just kept on grinning. He told them he was hungry and they headed over to Randy's Ribs, to eat.

As they got seated in a booth and were looking at the menu, Jimmy felt real nervous. He'd put on some cologne that morning and was dressed in a button up shirt and jeans. The outfit cost him nine dollars at the Goodwill. It was a special occasion; this was his first time in a real restaurant in eight years.

Skyler was across from him and he was staring at her. She was beautiful with her delicate features and long blonde ponytail. He made a mental note to get the old photo albums out of storage and look at his late mother's picture. Sky resembled her.

Bo was starting to get whiskers on his smooth boyish face and all of a sudden Jimmy saw himself in the boy.

"You know Bo, you are starting to look like I did at your age. I bet you will be taller though." Bo just grinned at him.

"So, have you gotten to drive much yet?" he asked. Bo looked over at Rose.

"I was hoping to try and take my test this week sometime, if Grandma has time to take me. I've studied that book every night for weeks."

Rose just gave him a noncommittal look. She wasn't ready, but she knew Bo was. There seemed to be a pause in the conversation, so Rose started to chatter about the weather.

"I sure hope it doesn't rain tomorrow. I'm planting tomatoes in the garden."

Bo laughed at her. "Grandma," he said, "You said you were planting last Monday."

"I guess I did." she grinned back at him. "You can both help me when you get home, I'll be out there. Watch and see."

They were laughing and cutting up through dinner and it was almost time to see the show. They were seeing a movie called 'End of the World'. It was supposed to keep you on the edge of your seat. Jimmy realized it would be the first time in eight years that he had popcorn. That in its self was a reason to be happy, and he was.

About halfway into the movie, Rose excused herself to visit the Ladies room. She was washing her hands and looking at her self in the mirror. She'd done a really good deed in her mind, letting the kids spend time with their dad. It would all work out, she had to have faith. She needed to give God this worry right now.

She started talking to God for a minute, praying to herself in the mirror, "God, help me to explain the things that are happening. Help me to understand them and keep my family safe. Watch over us Lord, in Jesus' name. Amen"

They were all sharing popcorn as she returned and it was offered to her. She sat munching as the movie droned on. She was barely absorbing the plot, as her thoughts roamed around in her mind. She was feeling good about the choices she made today; choosing to be here, choosing to forgive Jimmy.

Fear was there as well, churning in her gut. She was not going to allow the fear to overcome her. Something beyond her control or understanding was happening to Sky, and she needed to find a way to tell Jimmy what was going on.

They left the theatre and headed out to the parking lot laughing and talking all at once. There were throngs of people moving together, and as they moved through the exit to the parking lot, Jimmy had Sky's hand and Bo had his hand on Rose's arm.

Suddenly Jimmy let out a grunt and fell to the ground. Someone had Sky and she was being lifted. It was happening so fast and within a split second that seemed like five minutes, Skyler was being carried away.

Rose felt like she was in slow motion and could not move fast enough towards her granddaughter. She let out a scream "NOO!" and with her arm outstretched, she physically willed her body to catapult itself over to the child.

Skyler was thrown into a van and even before the side door was all the way shut, it was disappearing around a corner.

Bo ran after it. He was screaming, "SKY! SKYYYYYY!" but it kept going. Jimmy got up, grabbed his head, blinking rapidly to clear his vision and started to run after it as well. He had blood trickling down his face. He chased the white van until it reached the main road and increased speed. Then he ran back and grabbed his son.

"Are you okay, Son?"

Bo was in shock. "No. No, I'm not okay!" he was crying and shaking.

People were reacting and trying to help, but Rose was trying to get out of the throng. She was becoming hysterical and grabbed Bo. She said, "Someone call the police! Please, my granddaughter has been taken!" Then she felt herself passing out and Bo was there. They were both wailing loudly and screaming, "Oh my God! Oh my God!"

Her worst fear was realized. Her precious baby girl Sky was gone. This was a nightmare. It seemed like an hour, but it was only ten minutes before the police came screaming into the parking lot.

Rose stood, huddling and crying; Bo and Jimmy supported her.

More police were gathering. Rose and Bo were taken into one ambulance, while Jimmy was taken into another.

Bo was more concerned about Sky than anything; he kept pointing in the direction of the van's departure, declaring loudly, "They went that way!"

Neither he nor Rose required medical attention, but Jimmy was banged up. They had him in the ambulance and were administering oxygen. They surmised that he had been hit with a tire iron, which rendered a nasty welt on his head. He had a two-inch gash as well, which required ten stitches to close.

The police were questioning the gathered witnesses and everyone saw the same thing. All in all, fourteen people saw both of the men that took Sky.

They gave pretty good descriptions. The driver was twenty-five to thirty years old, a Caucasian with a slender face and light hair. He had a goatee and wore sunglasses. The man, who hit Jimmy and took Sky, was African American with a medium to muscular build. He was approximately six feet tall. He wore a dark blue cap, and had a closely shorn beard. One witness noticed an *Old Navy* logo on the upper right breast pocket of his black t-shirt. He seemed to be older than the driver, maybe forty to forty-five.

The family was taken to the police department and ushered into a room that held a couch, table and a few small chairs. The FBI was called in and a detective was questioning Rose, Jimmy and Bo. They were first offered water, tea or coffee. All of them declined and Rose had become irate as they sat there.

"They could be taking her out of state by now. Isn't anybody trying to find my granddaughter?" She was inconsolable, as she repeated the question several times.

The Chief of Police had been watching them from afar. He was letting the detectives handle it, but he watched the woman and felt compassion for her. He went into the room and sat down, introducing himself.

"Ms. England, we need you to stay calm. We want to take you all back to your home and await word. I'm aware of who you are. I need to ask you if you have any idea who would take your granddaughter?"

"No, Chief. Nobody." He began to tell her what they knew so far.

"The two men fit the descriptions of two former inmates recently paroled from prison. With descriptions given by witnesses, they've been tentatively identified as Daniel (Danny,) Banks, and Terrence (Terry,) Samuels. We're going to get them."

"Thank you, Chief. Please bring her home." He nodded, and patted her on the hand. Her face was ravaged from the ordeal. She was distraught and there was very little anyone could do to console her.

"You have my word we'll do everything we can. I need you to stay steady in case there is a ransom demand, okay?" Rose told him, "Okay."

Jimmy was pacing back and forth because he knew who they were. These two had targeted Sky while he was in the halfway house. They had commented on the Mercedes parked in the driveway, and asked him whose it was. Jimmy hadn't answered their questions. Now, he realized he'd been followed closely, as they planned to snatch his little girl.

Jimmy told the investigators that although he hadn't seen them, he felt it was definitely Samuels and Banks. He sat down, put his head in his hands and started to cry.

"Oh, God," he was praying out loud. "Please keep her safe, Lord. I swear I'll be the man you need me to be. I'll change. Oh, God, please keep her safe."

Rose had her hand on his back. She was a nervous wreck and as Annie arrived at the police station, Rose ran to her daughter and cried profusely.

Annie and Jimmy were face to face. After a quick acknowledgement, they hugged briefly.

"Oh, Annie, I'm so sorry." He was crying and his long wrenching sobs were too much for Rose to take. They were all distraught, but Bo, Annie and then Rose went over to Jimmy, consoling him and rubbing his shoulder.

Bo sat back down. He was stunned and couldn't believe his baby sister was gone. Convicts that knew his dad had taken her. He just looked around him and was trying hard to maintain a semblance of calm. He was listening to a lead detective explain what they knew.

The men, Mr. Banks and Mr. Samuels, had obviously seen Rose, and surmised there would be money for the girl's return.

The family was told to trust the investigation. It was time to go to the compound and await contact. Within thirty minutes the equipment would be in place to monitor and trace incoming calls.

Rose prayed to herself, "Father, please let them call. I'll do anything, just please let them call. I don't care how much they want. Lord I'll give everything to you. I'll send it all to the church, just please let them call."

Her prayers were answered within one hour of the family arriving at the compound. Two cars carrying a squadron of detectives piled in, and in a flurry of activity they had everything ready, when the phone rang.

Carla, the housekeeper answered, "England residence"

A garbled voice said, "Put the moneybag on." Her eyes got huge and her mouth was trembling. She was asking a silent question to the detective standing immediately in front of her, and he nodded his head in Rose's direction. Carla handed over the phone.

"This is Rose England. Please don't hurt my granddaughter. You can have anything you want. Please!"

A voice said, "Glad you feel that way, Lady. She sure is a purty thing. You need to wire $1 million to an account. Are you ready? You got 2 seconds to get a pen. One…………two. Credit and Loan Bank, account #426-887-592-845. Lady, you got till noon tomorrow and if you have not done what I ask, you'll never see your little princess again!" Then, the line went dead.

Jimmy, Annie and Bo came over to Rose and held her as they all sobbed together. It was 9:15PM.

"I have to go." Rose was crying. "I have to figure this out. Oh, Dear Lord, help me."

The lead detective stepped forward and told Rose to calm down. He started to talk to her matter of factly.

"Listen, Ms. England, we'll take it from here. We have money being funneled to the account as we speak. We'll need you to stay near the phone. This is a federal case, Ma'am; we'll need everyone to stay here. No one will be able to come or go, until we have found your granddaughter. We're going to do everything we can to get these guys and find her."

The detective went to the group of suits assembled in the corner and talked for three minutes. Then, he returned to the hysterical family on the sofa.

"Folks, this is always harrowing. We can only hope that these guys will not harm your loved one. I wish I could tell you something to reassure you, but I can only tell you that we'll use every technology available to set up surveillance around the bank in question. If he goes to retrieve or tries to electronically transfer the money, we'll get him."

Rose was trying to have faith. She was still praying under her breath, continuously.

Jimmy was having a real bad case of the jitters. When he thought of how he'd exposed Sky to this trash, he felt like scum. God help him, he had allowed her to be seen by these ex-cons when he let them come to the halfway house. He didn't think he could continue to live if they hurt her.

Annie had a hold of Bo. She was crying on her son's shoulder, making sounds that indicated her deep anguish. She'd never really bonded with the kids in all these years. She'd taken it for granted that she had two kids, never tending to them, never really putting them first. In her need for excitement and a fast lifestyle, she'd left them to be raised by her wealthy mother.

There was a lot of guilt spread around, but for Bo, it was devastation. Matilda had come in and was cocking her head at him. He knew the dog was wondering where her young mistress was. Bo started crying all over again, *Damn it, he had failed to protect her. He would kill that guy who took her. He would kill them both!*

Bo went into the kitchen and opened the cupboard. He needed something to calm him, so he reached for the cocoa mix. Grandma always made him cocoa when he wasn't feeling good; he reached for the comfort of the familiar can.

Jimmy came in and sat at the counter. He was a wreck and his head was bandaged up where the gash was. He was starting to get a shiner as well over his right eye. What a mess he'd created. He looked at Bo and started to talk, but Bo held up his hand and said, "I can't talk to you right now okay? I just can't talk right now."

The man who had been gone from him for eight years just nodded his head. The tears trickled down his face as he watched his son struggle to cope with this nightmare.

7
Sleepless Nights

Skyler was in a chair in a motel room. She only knew they had driven near the city and it had taken about an hour. She wasn't sure in what direction, but she felt they were headed to Illinois.

They made her stay back in a corner of the van's interior. She was blindfolded with a bandana of some sort and told to lie still. They told her to be quiet and don't try anything funny.

She obeyed for the most part, but she knew that she needed to listen, and try to figure out where she was being taken. She bent her head a certain way and found that she had a sliver if vision out the rear side window above her. She saw skyscrapers. That and the sound of traffic told her they were probably traveling through the city.

It was pitch black out now, and the traffic noises were gone. She felt the van traversing over gravel for a minute, and then it was moving backward and finally to a stop.

They had backed up to a motel room, located in a very quiet area south of the city of St. Louis. As the double rear doors of the van swung open, Sky was carried into the room and put in a chair. Again, she was warned to be quiet. The van pulled away and she was left with just one man, Terry Samuels.

She stared at the guy that sat on the bed. He told her she was going to get to go home, as soon as her rich granny paid the money. He told her he had a gun and she would die real fast if she made a sound.

Sky was feeling sick. Her stomach was tied up in knots and she was fighting the fear. She was thirsty as well. She asked the man if she could have some water. He told her, "Yea," filled a paper cup and handed it to her. She was trying real hard to gauge the danger with him. He didn't seem to have an aggressive nature toward her, and slowly she felt herself relax. Her muscles were all tensed up from the ordeal, and she wanted to stretch but remained there in the chair.

"Can I please have a pillow?" she asked him. He flung one over to her.

"Thanks, what's your name Mister?" He just looked at her and then went to the window. He wanted her to be quiet. He needed to think. She really was a cute little girl; he hoped they didn't have to hurt her.

"Your family will pay for you to come back right? I mean we know the old coot has money. She probably has millions. I just hope she can get a lot of it together fast. If not, sorry, Charlie."

"I don't know why you're doing this. Money isn't everything. You'll probably get caught, you know." He turned to her then, continuing the steady low back and forth. They'd only been here an hour, but it seemed like eight.

"Listen, kid, I don't want to hurt you. I'm a convict and there aren't too many jobs out there for me. I can never get a nice house or a nice car. I sure hope your granny pays up, cause then I can go somewhere and eat good food. Prison food is horrible, I wouldn't feed my dog some of the stuff we got fed."

Skyler asked him again what his name was.

"You can just call me Mister," he said. "Best that you and I do not become friends."

"Did you know my dad when you were in jail?" she asked him.

"No, I don't know your old man. Kid, you need to chill out cause this is a waiting game we got here."

Sky just sat there looking at him. She wasn't afraid he would hurt her, but she didn't know about the other guy. She was thinking about her family and she missed them. They were probably real worried. If only he would let her call home, maybe they would know she was okay. She watched him a minute, waiting for the courage to speak up again. The silence grew as he stared at the TV watching some Arnold Schwarzenegger movie.

"Do you think it would be okay if I called my grandmother to let her know I'm okay?"

"No." he said. "We have to wait now, till we hear about the money. Your granny just needs to concentrate on getting that done. That's all we want kid, just the money."

Sky felt so deflated. She knew Bo would try and find her as well as her grandma. She also knew that her grandmother loved her very much and would give the people money if she could.

Matilda was probably wondering where she was. The little dog was very attached to her. She was always waiting for her on the bed when she arrived home from school. Every day, she got greeted with tiny little kisses from the puppy. She felt herself start to cry.

It was getting late now, and she felt sleepy. She was thinking that soon something would happen, as it had been a couple of hours since she was brought here. Her captor was still channel surfing so she closed her eyes. She had seen this happen last night but she wasn't able to stop it.

She couldn't sleep and felt her stomach growl. She asked him if there was any food.

"Kid, you are becoming a pain in my ass! Why can't you just be quiet and let me concentrate?" Sky did not back down.

"I was just asking. I'm hungry and I can't sleep."

Terry Samuels was beginning to regret his decision to participate in this. It had all sounded so easy as Banks outlined the plan. There was supposed to be a ransom demand and after it was delivered, they would put the kid out on their way to Canada.

They had agreed they would not hurt the girl. Terry had two little girls in Mississippi. He would never have agreed to be in on it, if he thought they were going to hurt the kid.

So, it was on. The ransom call should have been made by now. He wondered if it had gone down as planned and if they had tried to trace it. He just needed to lay low till tomorrow at noon. Then Banks was supposed log in at the coffee shop. From there, he would make an electronic transfer as soon as the funds were released. It could take more time, but Terry was supposed to hold the girl and wait.

He'd thought about this for weeks now. The options were scarce for a convict. It was a life that moved very slowly. He had time, but now, as he sat in the room with the kid, he realized that he was not cut out for this kind of gig. If he couldn't keep her quiet, he was going to lose his patience. The walls were already starting to close in on him and it had only been a few hours.

Skyler just sat there; she looked from him to the T.V. and back at him again. He was feeling like he needed to go outside and smoke a cigarette just to unwind and get some air.

"Hey, I'm going right out here to smoke. When I get back, I'll figure out something for food okay? Sit tight and don't make any noise. Got it?" He looked at her, asking with his eyes if she would cooperate.

Skyler nodded her head and told him she had to go in the bathroom.

"Okay, but don't make me look for you. Make it snappy."

Samuels was trying real hard to stay calm. Years back when he was just a whippersnapper he'd robbed some houses. The adrenaline he felt as he crawled around in some strange house was like having a heart attack. He lay down outside in the woods after it was done. His heart was racing one hundred miles an hour. He hadn't liked the feeling then, and this was even worse. He was shaking, fidgeting and he felt like he needed to chain smoke the entire pack of Marlboros.

If he could just get through this, he could start over somewhere nice and quiet. Maybe he could go see his girls someday, bring them a birthday present, have ice cream and do normal things, like go to the zoo. He vowed that he was going to be good to them, if it took him his whole life. He would do something that would make them proud of him...proud that he was their dad.

He had to figure out the food situation. In the joint, you had three square meals. He was used to eating at 7 AM, 12 PM and again at 5 PM. He needed to call for pizza. There was a coupon on the bedside table. Hopefully the kid liked pizza, cause that was all he was going to be able to come up with.

Skyler had found the remote. She was watching a movie about Tom Hanks getting stranded on an island. In the film, he was befriending a soccer ball. She saw him draw a face on it and could relate to the feeling of needing a companion. She decided that she would try and befriend her captor.

"Do you like pizza, kid?" he asked her.

"Yes, that would be great. I like pepperoni and extra cheese please." She gave him a smile. He eyed her, not trusting her cheerful response.

Samuels called it in and gave them the address. He had some money in his pocket so he dug it out. He took his perch on the bed again, waiting for the knock.

"Mister, how long do you think it will be before I can go home?" Skyler asked him.

He looked at her. She was such a bright-eyed little thing. He thought about his two girls and how he would feel if something like this happened to them. He decided that he would be gentle and try to waylay her fears.

"I don't know, kid. It all depends on your granny getting the money over to where we told her to take it. We will know more tomorrow. We got nothing we need to do, so just relax and enjoy your little stay. I don't want to hurt you kid. I just need money. As long as you do what I tell you, it's all going to be okay."

Skyler nodded her head and looked back at the television, where Tom Hanks was shouting over a huge fire he'd just built. It was a riveting scene and she felt herself drawn into the feeling that he had conquered the challenge.

The pizza came. Samuels thanked the guy and paid him. As they were eating, he watched her, and she him. A quiet camaraderie was developing. Skyler needed consoling so she decided to start talking to him.

"Thanks, this is really good. We used to have pizza night all the time at my house. Grandma said it was just for special times, so I guess I kind of feel like this is special somehow. Thanks for getting extra cheese, it's really yummy." She smiled one of her best smiles at him, choosing to be kind to her captor.

He told her she was welcome. The way she made him feel was something he hadn't felt in a long time. She was just so sweet and accepting of him as a person. It was the same kind of sweet accepting nature that his little gals had.

"I got two girls close to your age," He decided to keep it brief, but he was kind of enjoying the child. "I haven't seen them in four years, but I have a few pictures. Would you like to see them?"

Skyler, who sat vigorously chewing, nodded, "Sure," she said. "How old are they?"

Samuels started to relax finally, Sky could tell. He sat back a little wiping his mouth off.

"Shellie girl is 11, and Cassie is 9. They are real sweet little girls, and smart. Their momma takes them to dance lessons. I got pictures of them in their little costumes." He dug in his pocket, pulled out a raggedy wallet and flipped it open to two grainy snapshots. He pointed to the dark haired girl on the left.

"This is Cassie." He was smiling now, and Skyler made a mental note that it was a nice look for him. He continued to gaze lovingly at the photos.

"You remind me of Cassie a little. She's got bright eyes like yours. This one's Shellie girl, she looks just like her old man. They are such good girls."

Skyler was listening and she asked where they were.

"Oh," he told her "They stay with their momma, pretty far away from here."

"Mister, if you go back to prison, you won't ever get to see them. Don't you want to see them grow up?" Skyler was asking him an honest question. She was staring at him, her brows knit with confusion. "Why would you do something that will make you go back?"

"You don't understand what it's like for a man to have nothing, not even his pride. I don't have a bank account or a car. This is a chance to start fresh somewhere. We'll both have money to start over, get a job and have some kind of life. You can't take care of anybody, if you can't even take care of yourself." He was silent for several minutes.

"I'm done telling you stuff, kid. Let's get some sleep, it's getting real late." He threw a blanket her way and she pulled it up over her.

Skyler snuggled down into the chair, leaving the bed open for the man. She was thinking about their conversation and how he had little girls around her age. She saw him as a person now, not so much as a kidnapper. She was still confused about why a guy would do something so horrible.

As she started to nod off, she was imagining Matilda cuddled up to her. She rarely slept without her little pet. It wasn't scary here anymore, but she was still worried about her family. They were probably pretty upset about her abduction from the theatre. She wished she could let them know she was okay.

It was in the still early morning that she woke up. She'd seen a vision and it was vivid and real. She lie there a moment, getting her bearings. When she replayed what she had just envisioned, she started to cry and looked toward the window wondering why. The curtains moved gently from the air conditioner flow. Skyler rose and went over to gaze out. It was a pitch-black night. Nothing moved except a few bugs around a dimly lit street lamp. She was so lonely right now. She needed her grandma.

She was becoming more alert and realized that what she had seen would happen in a few hours. She knew she had to wake the man up and tell him about it. He might not believe her, but she knew there was no other choice.

Her voice was frozen in her throat, but she croaked out, "Mister, Mister," and "Wake up, Mister!" she didn't venture close, but was standing about three feet from the bedside.

Samuels woke up and looked at the clock.

"What in the world are you caterwauling about girl? My Lord, it's only 4 AM! How's a guy supposed to get any sleep with you making such a fuss? What did you do, have a nightmare?"

"Mister, I heard shots and there's blood! She's screaming and crying and there are sirens. It's going to happen today. We have to do something. Do you hear me, Mister? We have to do something now to stop it from happening!" Skyler was standing there with her hair sticking up and he needed to try and calm her down.

"Listen to me kid. You've had a nightmare and I don't understand what it was about. Now listen, everything's okay here I'm not going to hurt you, you're safe. I need you to go lie down and go back to sleep."

She persisted, "No, you have to do something. I saw blood and she's screaming!"

"Who's screaming? Whose blood? Kid, I need some rest, for God's sake!" He was losing patience with her. He was still half asleep and didn't want to listen to this right now. God, why did everything have to be such a pain in his ass?

Samuels sat up then. He was trying to wake up, and he shook his head a little to clear the cobwebs. He looked at her, and realized that she was really upset.

Skyler was just staring at some point above his head. He asked her again, "What are you saying? Whose blood?" A tear was sliding slowly down Skyler's face. She was staring at something distant. It was an image in her mind that no one else could see.

She tried to describe the vision.

"I saw a bus stop. It's going to happen in the bus stop. She's bleeding, the kids are crying, and someone's trying to do CPR on her."

Skyler finally focused on the man sitting there on the bed. She was weeping fully now, because the horror of seeing the bullet thump into the little girl's body had jolted her awake. It was immediately apparent to her, that she'd just seen that face in a grainy photo.

"Mister, sometimes I see bad stuff before it happens. It's the little girl in the picture. She's at a bus stop and it's morning. A car is driving by and shooting at someone in another car. A bullet is going to hit her, but we have time. We can stop it because it hasn't happened yet."

Samuels was completely perplexed by the words coming out of this little girl's mouth. Her eyes were penetrating into his consciousness and he was fully awake now. He blinked his eyes for a few seconds digesting what she was telling him. It was beyond his comprehension, but he felt like what she was saying was true.

"So, let me get this straight. You saw my little girl get shot?" he was incredulous.

"Sometimes, I see things before they happen. I don't know why, but you have to believe me, Mister. You have to stop it somehow."

He stared at her a moment. There was such a sense of urgency in her face as she peered at him, and suddenly he felt it. He felt a gut instinct to protect the girls from whatever unseen danger they were in. He was going to act on it.

With a second of hesitancy, he looked long and hard at Skyler's face. He couldn't fathom that what she was saying was true, but he wasn't willing to risk it.

He picked up the phone and dialed a number. Skyler stood stock still, listening, watching and willing him to do something that would change the events she had foreseen.

"Momma, yea Momma it's me, Terry. Yea, I'm out. Yea, I know it's only four in the morning. Momma, I need you to call Sandra for me. Tell her to keep the girls away from the bus stop today. Please, Momma, this is important. She can drive them to school, or have someone take them, but tell her not to let them go to the bus stop shelter. There's some kind of gang threat. Now, I need you to promise me you'll call Sandra right after you hang up. I wish I could call her, but she won't answer unless she sees your number."

On the other end, an old woman sat up in bed and grabbed her robe. She stared at the phone a moment after she put it back in its cradle. She was sifting through the things she'd just heard her son say. There was no hesitation, as she opened the drawer in the bedside table, and got out the tiny address book.

After two rings, the voice on the other end of the line was scratchy and barely coherent. "Yes."

"Sandra, it's Donna. I need you to listen to me a minute. Terry just called, and he said there's going to be some gang activity in town this morning. He made me call you, to tell you the girls must stay away from the bus stop."

The other end of the line was silent for a second, as the young woman realized that her two little girls could be in some kind of danger. The conversation was short but effective. A man in prison has ears on the wall, and if he called her at four AM to say there was some kind of gang threat, she was definitely going to act on it.

Sandra did not hesitate to reassure her mother-in-law that she would drive the girls to school today. She told her not to worry, and to call her later that afternoon, so they could talk.

Both women were perplexed to say the least, but when it came to the two children, there wasn't anything they wouldn't do to keep them safe.

Wide-awake in the dark motel room, Terry Samuels sat up with his head in his hands. It had to be a bad dream, triggered by all of the trauma of being taken. He hoped so because the alternative was unspeakable. She'd seen something happen that could destroy him.

What kind of psychic ability did this little girl have? He'd never seen anything like it before.

He was afraid to go to sleep; afraid she would awaken him again. He got up, and put on some coffee. It was going to be a long day. He sent a furtive glance to her still form.

Skyler's eyes were growing heavy again. She didn't want to see anything else. God had given her these visions to save people, but here she was, in the room with a kidnapper. It suddenly occurred to her that if he hadn't taken her, a little girl would be shot and killed in a few hours. She was relieved that he'd done something to stop what she'd seen happen. The vision had been chilling. Now, she was afraid to go back to sleep, for fear of having another one.

8

Redemption

There was another nightmare going on at the compound in the hills. It was a waiting game, as the surveillance team physically and electronically monitored the Credit and Loan bank account. Any activity requested would be flagged, and its location would be revealed.

The technology would send an automatic GPS trace into effect. Even in the event that a remote computer was used to initiate the activity, it would ping the nearest tower and be located within four minutes of the keystroke.

They waited, pacing a worn path into the carpet. They drank coffee, tea, and ate small sandwiches prepared by Carla. The odds were in their favor that Skyler Conrad was alive. They were just waiting now for the deposit to be cleared for withdrawal and the transaction to take place. The ball was in the kidnappers' court.

Even though it was a new account and would not technically be activated for twenty-four hours, the bank had been swayed to allow the deposit to be immediately available for withdrawal. The branch was in a special quarantine as well. There were six people inside; the branch manager and five FBI agents.

Outside, there were eight more team members standing vigilant, complete with bulletproof vests. The area was cordoned off to any traffic, pedestrian or otherwise, and they were on alert from any movement from ground or sky.

At the compound, it was just after nine AM. Rose, Annie, Jimmy, and Bo were in the kitchen. No one had slept, not even the dogs. They continued to cling to Rose and Bo, instinctually guarding their masters. They sensed something was wrong, letting out several low growls at the squads of people wandering through.

The kidnappers had maintained radio silence through the night. It was assumed that they were readying themselves to initiate the bank withdrawal and getaway. If the police had a say they would both be caught dead or alive after Skyler was located. Every resource was being used to see that she came home safe.

An FBI profiler entered the kitchen and strode over to Rose. He had gathered a lot of pertinent information on both men, and was filling her in on some favorable facts.

One of the kidnappers, Terrance Samuels, had two little girls in Mississippi. He had served five years for burglary, and other petty thefts. He was not a violent predator, and had never served time for violent crimes.

Daniel Banks was not such a good guy. He had served eight years of a fifteen-year sentence for attempted murder. He had a rap sheet that revealed several charges for violent crimes. The only real good thing here was that neither of the men had ever been arrested for crimes against a child, physically or sexually.

Rose took comfort in that. They were still monsters in her mind, but she prayed that somewhere in their hearts, they would be gentle in their treatment of Skyler.

Daniel Banks watched the clock. He was holed up in an old house on the outskirts of town. He was so agitated he hadn't slept at all last night. The radio silence was agreed upon, but he wondered how Samuels was doing with the kid. It was only 9:45 AM, but he needed a beer.

The coffee shop, his next destination in the plan, was a half-mile away. He had it all figured out. The van had been ditched into an outbuilding, which barely contained the boxy vehicle. He had crawled to the back to exit the sliding door, because the driver's side door would not open far enough to let him out.

He'd leased a blue 1999 Pontiac Firebird from the car dealer in Belleville a few months back. It was stashed in the garage a few feet away, gassed up and ready to go.

Banks was waiting for noon to arrive. He would log on, transfer the money, and hightail it to get Samuels and the girl. He felt real good about the odds of it all going down without a hitch. Even if they traced his location, it would take them a while to get here and by then, he'd be long gone.

Everything had to go like clockwork for them to pull this off. He planned to transfer the funds to an account he'd set up in Canada, and then he was going to have his old friend Kyle Thornton get it out for him. He promised a $50k paycheck for the little deed. It was a good plan. He'd spent a lot of time in that old ramshackle halfway house figuring it out.

Ten years back, before his conviction, he used to work on a freighter that traveled up and down the Mississippi River. He had a few friends waiting for his call. He would drive out of state and board a freighter going north, leaving no trace. He had to be real quick in retrieving Samuels and the kid.

Samuels would come with him, but would return home after a few years. If they could just pull this off, it would be sweet dreams from here on out.

Banks was trying to figure out if that dip shit Jimmy Conrad, hadeven gotten a look at him. That was the only way they could be identified. If they could just get out of town before the cops figured out who they were, they might make it. The idea was to avoid checkpoints. Danny knew the odds were against them, but what a payroll they would have if they made it to Canada.

He was going to dye his hair black and grow a big bushy beard and Terry Samuels was going to shave his head and get some tattoos. They had talked about different ways to completely disguise their identities once they were free and clear, with eyeglasses and hats.

Back at the motel, Samuels was eating some cold pizza. Skyler was snoozing in the chair and he was flipping through stations. He listened for keywords before moving on. Words like: kidnapper, convicts, search, or ransom. He was still pretty shaken up about the surreal events that had gone down this morning, and the resulting phone call to his mother.

CNN was on, with some bizarre random news about mudslides and wildfires, but all of a sudden there was tickertape on the bottom of the screen about a gang shooting that seriously injured two children.

Samuels sat up in the bed and waited for it to roll again. He read it through. *Breaking News…two children in critical condition, seriously wounded as a result of a random shooting in rural Calvary, Mississippi. Possibly related to gang activity. Two suspects at large are being sought for questioning. Please call 1-800-suspects with any information.*

He just sat there a minute, absorbing the fact that what the girl dreamed had come true. It had happened.

His thoughts were a shocking sequence of questions. *'What? How did she know?'*

There were no answers for him, and as he glanced over at her he felt some kind of dam open up inside of him. He started to cry. She had saved his babies' lives and here he was holding her for ransom. She was so sweet; her parents must be crushed with worry.

Five minutes went by, and Terry was coming to grips with the fact that he had no clue about the little girl he had here. He was shaken by the events as he stood looking at her all curled up in the chair; he knew he'd kill somebody if they took his child. God help him, he couldn't be a part of this anymore.

Terry Samuels was about to do something that took more courage than he'd ever shown in his 37 years of life. He was going to give up, and set Skyler free. If he got shot, it would be more than he deserved. It was the only right thing to do. She had saved his kids.

He stepped out of the room a minute to figure out his plan. He lit a cigarette and took a few long pulls before flicking it away. He still had a few hours of radio silence, which would end once the money went into the Canadian account. He went back inside, picked up the phone, and made another call to the familiar number.

"Momma, hi, yea, me again. I saw on the news. Yea, I know, I'm sure glad you picked up the phone. Listen, Mom, I've been involved in some real bad stuff. I need to ask you a favor. Whatever you hear or see, don't worry, okay? I'm probably going back in real soon, and I just need you to tell my girls I love them."

On the other end, his mother told him she loved him too. He told her the favor he needed was for her to please forgive him. She told him, of course she would. Nothing he could ever do would make her love him any less. Then she hung up, and he just stood there, feeling his heart open up and pour out onto the wine colored carpeting.

After a deep cleansing cry, Terry Samuels went over and woke the sleeping child. She wasn't even scared as she looked at him.

"Morning, Mister," she said. Her eyes looked like two pieces of crystal as they glittered in the sunlight flowing into the shadowy room. She grinned trustingly up at him.

That's when he knew his decision to free her had been the right one. Maybe this would be the final act he could take some pride in, some self-respect. He told her she was going home and it was over.

"Really? You're letting me go home?" she asked.

"Yea, what you did for me was pretty amazing. I can't keep you here any more. I'm calling the police, kid. Don't be scared okay? It's going to get crazy and I'm going to be taken away in handcuffs. I want you to know I'm grateful to you for saving Shellie and Cassie from that gunfire. It happened this morning just like you said. Two kids were shot and are in the hospital. They could die. This is something I'll never forget."

Skyler stood up then, combed her hands through her hair and said, "I'm glad they're okay, but I wished no one had been in the bus stop. I'm really sad about that." She paused, "I can't wait to go home. I really want my grandma. Thanks, Mister." Then she smiled at him and it was one of the most beautiful things he'd seen in years. She had to be some kind of an angel.

He started crying again, but this time it was joyful and freeing.

He felt like a weight had lifted off of his shoulders and he wanted to get down on his knees and thank God.

Samuels took a deep calming breath and went over to the phone to make the call. He told the dispatcher who he was, and that he had Skyler Conrad safe and secure. He told them he was surrendering, and gave them his address.

Within three minutes, they both heard the sirens. Skyler came over and asked him for a hug. He told her he was sorry for taking her, and he would never forget her. Her eyes mesmerized him, as he asked her to forgive him. She gave a nod as they embraced and went to the door.

The loud voice outside said, "Come out with your hands up, now!" He looked at her and gave her a tiny grin through his tears. Then he closed his eyes, said a silent prayer and walked outside.

Samuels put his hands up in the air. A multitude of cops continued to arrive, the gravel flew as their cars skidded to a stop. There was a flurry of shouts and in a frenzy of activity they swarmed towards Skyler and she was ushered into a vehicle.

He lay on his stomach handcuffed, with much more than just a pistol aimed at him. He turned his head, trying to see Skyler. He needed to see her sweet face once more. She was in the car and their eyes met briefly. It was something that would forever change him as she signed, 'I love you' pointing first to her eye, then her heart and then at him. It was just exactly the way his baby girls did it, and it broke him.

The officers were told to transport him immediately to FBI headquarters, twenty-two miles away.

In the small town of Eureka, an urgent phone call came into the Chief of Police. The child was safe. He thought about the woman he'd met last night. He was haunted by her cries for her granddaughter, and he'd prayed last night for Skyler's safe return. He would personally cruise past her home tonight. For some reason, she stayed on his mind.

They began questioning Terry Samuels in the squad car. He spilled his guts about everything. He told them where to find Banks and the plan to let Skyler out on the road to Canada. He was feeling pretty good actually. He realized that no one knew what she'd done. He'd witnessed a miracle. He'd been given a gift to be in her presence.

Daniel Banks was not expecting the barrage of police that were coming at him. He was sitting on the porch of the old shack smoking a cigarette and enjoying his second beer, when he saw the first flashing cherry coming down the road.

It was 10:15 AM. His first instinct was denial. They had to be heading on down the road, they weren't coming here, no, he was in the clear.

It was a convoy, and the flashing cherries were increasing in numbers. There were four squad cars speeding towards him with sirens silenced. They were coming hard and fast.

He got up, threw his beer bottle across the railing and high-tailed it inside. His heart was about to burst out of his chest and fly right through his denim shirt.

Daniel Banks was in trouble and he knew it. He cocked the shotgun and put it to the window, aiming it at the closest patrol car.

"Come out with your hands up, Banks!" He was sweating profusely.

"It's all over! We got the girl and Samuels. You need to come on out here; we don't want bloodshed, Danny."

"I don't believe you, you're bluffing."

"No, we aren't bluffing, Danny. We knew right where you were because Terry told us. Now we're giving you exactly one minute to open the door and come out with your hands up. Do as we say, and you won't get hurt. Countdown starts now."

Danny Banks didn't want to die. Out of the corner of the window, he saw at least eight guns pointing at him and knew he had one choice, prison or death.

"I'm coming out, don't shoot!" He put down the shotgun, going to the door. He pushed it open and stepped out onto the porch with his hands up.

He was barely one step out when he felt them coming. They got his hands behind his back; he was cuffed and thrown down to the ground. They searched his pockets and he was carried over to the car and put in. They had him face down on the backseat, his feet tied together.

As a swarm of police gathered around the car, Banks heard them talking about Skyler.

"She's fine. By the grace of God, we got both kidnappers and she is being returned to her family as we speak. Good job, people."

He lay there with his face smashed into the gray tweed seat. He was going back in. After six months of freedom, he was going back to his former home of steel bars and the smell of rotting humanity.

Thirty-five miles to the west, a car was traveling towards the foothills of the Ozark Mountains. Skyler sat in the back with a female police officer. She was staring out the window, watching the terrain change. The road was winding into shadowed forests, filled with woodland creatures. It was a familiar countryside, so opposite of the city, and Skyler never realized how much she loved it.

The lady on her right was Sergeant Betty D'Angelo. She was chatting about the bluffs along the river.

"This is gorgeous country out here. We used to float on the Merrimac River every summer. Were you born here Skyler?"

Skyler was listening with half of an ear, but she was about to jump out of her skin with excitement as the miles flew by and she got closer to home.

"I've lived here since I was a tiny baby. It's the only place I remember." Sgt. D'Angelo nodded and smiled at the little girl.

As she sipped at her bottle of water, and watched for familiar landmarks, Skyler could only think about home and Terry Samuels. She was confused why a man would be so worried about getting money that he would get be involved with a kidnapping. It was something she just couldn't understand. Why was the need to have money so strong that a person would risk their freedom and end up back in jail?

As the miles flew behind them, they started climbing. Craggy hillsides and sheer drop offs with breathtaking views passed, as they wound upward. Finally they slowed, as the cruiser arrived at the gates of the compound. The gates were open, and as the car turned into the drive, people swarmed toward it, surrounding them.

Skyler jumped out as soon as they came to a stop and leapt into her grandmother's arms. They were sobbing and hugging tightly, and then it was Bo's turn. He got down on his knees, holding his sister tightly to his chest, crying and telling her how much he loved her.

She was beyond happy. It had been less than twenty-four hours, but it seemed like a week. She never wanted to leave home again. Then she heard a familiar cry and looked down; Matilda. She picked up the little dog and kissed her sweet head. Martin was there as well, jumping on her legs and barking as he ran circles, trying to get her attention. God had brought her home and all of her prayers had been answered.

Her father and mother rushed in as well, crying and reaching for their child. They were grateful she was home and needed reassurance that she was okay. Both of them had prayed for this moment. She was hugged for a full 5 minutes as her family cried with joy.

"Oh Skyler, we love you so much. Thank God you're okay. Did they hurt you baby?" Her mom was asking her questions, but she wasn't ready to talk about anything. She wanted to go in the house and go to her room. She needed to rest; it had been a very long night.

"Can I please have something to eat?" she asked. And then,

"Grandma, I'm so thirsty for a cup of your special cocoa."

"Of course sweetheart; let's get you inside now. Everyone, please give her some space. Come on Sweet, Carla will make you a sandwich."

The two police officers were done here. Sergeant D'Angelo went to Rose, handed her a card, and said, "Call me if you need anything."

Rose told her, "Thanks" and shook her hand. The sergeant saluted Skyler and told her to take care.

Rose gathered her granddaughter under her arm and turned, heading toward the house as the others followed. Bo watched as the gates closed behind the departing car, taking comfort in the fact that they would close and automatically lock.

Jimmy came over and picked his daughter up. He carried her all the way up the stairs, into the house, and then set her down very gently on the sofa, as if she were a porcelain doll. He and Annie just stood looking at her.

Annie was thinking she'd never realized how fragile Skyler was. She was only ten years old, and for her to have spent the night in a motel room with a kidnapper made Annie's blood freeze. She was searching for some signs of damage.

Skyler didn't understand why they were all acting funny. She was fine. The police had reassured them she had not been hurt, but they were still concerned for her. Annie came over and sat down beside her.

"Honey, was the man mean to you?" she asked, as she gently pushed Skyler's hair away from her eyes.

"No, he was nice actually, and by this morning, we were kind of like friends. He has two little girls himself." She was thinking she needed to tell her grandma what happened this morning. Her mother knew about her visions as well, but Skyler wanted Rose.

Jimmy didn't know about her special gift yet. He would be told soon. Nobody else beyond the family except Matthew Roads knew about the visions in her dreams. Skyler was wondering if her dad was ready to hear about them.

She smiled at her mom. "Were you worried about me, Mom?" she asked her.

"I've never been so scared about anything in my whole life Skyler. Your dad and I stayed up all night worried about you. We prayed in the chapel with Granny and Bo last night. I guess God has answered our prayers once again." Annie wiped tears away and blew her nose hard into a tissue.

Skyler was so happy. She hugged her mom and kissed her on the cheek. "I'm okay now, Mommy. Don't cry."

Jimmy couldn't take it anymore; he lost it and started sobbing. Bo went over to him saying softly, "It's okay to cry Dad; it's God's way of letting all the hurt and pain be washed away."

Rose stood watching and suddenly she realized that every time a horrible event happened in her family, it brought them all together and it brought them all home. First Annie getting kidnapped brought her home, and now Jimmy was here. As dysfunctional as they were, Jimmy and Annie were part of the family.

As she brought in the cup of cocoa and a plate with sandwiches on it, she said, "Sky, tomorrow, we have to go downtown to make a statement to the police. I will stay with you through it all. For now, I am beefing up security around here to keep the news stations away. How are you feeling, Sweetheart? Are you tired?"

"I'm really tired." She continued to chew but never took her eyes off of her grandmother. "I stayed up talking to the man real late last night, then I woke up at four in the morning." Rose looked at her and saw something odd in her expression.

"Any particular reason you were awake that early, Sky? Tell me the truth, he didn't hurt you in any way did he?"

Skyler shook her head.

"No, he wasn't like that. I'm thinking I'd like to take a nap now. Will you lay with me awhile? I didn't think I was that tired but now that I'm home, it's all catching up to me."

Rose was picking up some subtle hints that Skyler needed to talk to her about something. She had a feeling it was some kind of vision. What in the world could she have seen that had convinced him to let her go?

An hour later, Rose was hearing a tale that made the hairs on the back of her neck stand up. The vision Skyler had was of a drive by shooting in Mississippi. She had convinced her kidnapper, Mr. Samuels, to make a call that kept his two little girls from the bus stop this very morning. It was all so unbelievable. Rose was having a hard time taking it all in.

After holding her close and assuring her that she was safe now, Rose got up, patted the dogs on their cute little heads and left the room. After they finished at the police station tomorrow, Rose wanted to go see Matthew Roads. She needed someone to document the statements Sky was making. Meanwhile, she needed to have a family meeting.

They were all there in the kitchen sitting around the table when Rose came down. Carla, Bo, Annie, and Jimmy all stopped talking and stood still as they waited for Rose to tell them how she was.

"She's really fine." Rose told them, and suddenly her face just crumpled and she had to sit down a minute. Through her tears, she started to tell them about the kidnapper.

"Skyler was in the back of the van on the floor, she said she was told to keep quiet. Last night she slept in a chair in the motel room. She told me he shared pizza with her and showed her pictures of his two daughters. She told me he was not a bad man."

Rose wanted to share more with her family about Skylers vision. She made the decision that now would be a good time. It was almost 3 PM, and with Skyler safely upstairs sleeping, she might as well tell them everything.

"There's more. Let me get a cup of tea before I start." They all waited patiently, chattering quietly and looking at Rose. Finally she sat back down, and they quieted.

"Jimmy there's something about Skyler you need to know. Carla I know this is going to be shocking for you as well and hard to believe. Jimmy, do you believe in psychic abilities?"

He'd been petting the cat, but now he looked at her like she was talking gibberish.

"I don't know, yea, I guess it's possible. What's that got to do with Skyler?" He was getting a strange feeling that everyone else knew what she was talking about. He looked at Annie, and she looked down, then he looked at his son. Bo looked at Rose and gave her his full attention.

"Skyler has been having visions, Jimmy." She'd decided to just say it out right. "We've taken her to a specialist on psychic phenomena and it's incredibly rare. There are no cases like hers. She sees an event happen before it happens. Some may call it a premonition, but it's more like a vision because it's in a dream. She wakes up and is able to warn us. So far we've been able to take action to stop things from happening."

Jimmy was shaking his head. He didn't understand anything about supernatural stuff. He was one of the biggest skeptics anyone ever saw. Now, Rose was telling him that his little girl had some kind of psychic ability to see into the future.

"What the heck are you talking about? What is all this mumbo jumbo?"

"She's trying to tell you that Skyler sees things while she's asleep," Annie decided to try and explain it to Jimmy. "It's like a dream, but it's real. Whatever she sees is going to happen and she knows it. She sees it before it happens."

Annie started crying and had to take a moment. Then she continued on because Jimmy was listening and as far-fetched as it all sounded, he knew it was true.

"She saw me get abducted, Jimmy! She woke Mom up and insisted she call the police. It was beyond anything I've ever known. She saw it all. She saved my life and I will be forever changed." Annie grabbed his hand, saying softly, "We know it's hard to wrap your head around, but you're her dad, and she needs you to believe in her."

Rose needed to tell them what Skyler had told her upstairs.

"You all need to hear this. Something amazing happened in the motel room. Skyler had a vision of the kidnapper's little girl getting shot. Something about a gang shooting while the little one was in a bus stop."

They were all staring at her with their mouths open. "Oh my God, Mom!" Annie cried. "What happened?"

"Well," Rose continued. "Skyler woke him up and made him call his mother to warn his wife about the shooting. In her vision, she saw the bullet go into his little girl." Rose grabbed her tissue again, sniffling.

"Go on, Rose, what else happened?" Jimmy was shocked, but he needed to know everything.

"She went back to sleep after he made the phone call, then he saw it on the news this morning. That's when he made the decision to let her go. He saw that two kids were shot and in critical condition!" Rose swiped at her eyes and blew her nose. The story was incredulous, but then, so was everything else that happened in the past year.

"That is the craziest thing I've ever heard! Rose, how can this be? I can't believe this." Jimmy was blown away by what he'd just learned. At first he wanted to believe they were all under some kind of spell or maybe Skyler had fed them some fantasy. He was having a hard time swallowing all of this. His little girl was some kind of psychic?

"I want to go with you to see the doctor, Rose. I need to see and hear what is happening to Sky from here on out, okay?" He was so concerned about her that he forgot all about his problems.

"That's fine, Jimmy." Rose wanted him involved. She was grateful that he and Annie were here. She decided to do something that she hoped she would not regret.

"Jimmy, I want you to stay here with us. You can have the T.V. room off of the kitchen. I need all of us together through this. What do you say?" She reached out touching his shoulder. He was still shaking his head in wonderment of what he's just been told. He started crying.

"I don't deserve any of you. I'm so ashamed that I exposed all of you to those criminals. Oh God, I'm so grateful that she's home safe."

"She needs you. She needs all of us." Rose continued to touch his shoulder. "I've never asked you for anything Jimmy, but I'm asking now. Can you please promise me you'll be a father? I ask for her, because she's never known you. I'm asking you to never touch a drug again, to do something selfless and just give your life over to being a dad to both of them. What do you say?" Rose was asking something serious of him.

"I promise, Rose. I promise." He was nodding and tears were still rolling down his face unchecked through his grateful smile. "I thank you."

Bo got up and came over to the table where his Dad was sitting.

He just stared at him for a minute.

"If you hurt her and leave us for getting high again, you won't get another chance. I got to protect her, you know. Every since I was six, I've protected her." Bo's lips were quivering now as he fought with his emotions. He was flexing his fists, angry with his father.

"Bo, I'm so sorry. The old me was just a punk kid. I promise things are going to be different now. I'll prove it to you. You are the best brother a girl could ask for you know? I'm so proud of you." He stood up and hugged his son. Bo, who had been stiff at first, suddenly released his shoulders, allowing the hug. He continued to listen to his grandmother address his mom.

"Annie, I'm trusting you to do exactly what I just asked of Jimmy. Do you think I'm asking too much?"

"No, Mom. It's time we put the kids first, way past time actually. I'm so sorry Mom. God I've been so horrible. I don't deserve you guys, Bo." Bo smiled at his mom.

"It's okay. She's okay, and we have another chance to do what's right in this family." Bo was seeing his parents for the people he remembered. They were his mom and dad again. They were here to stay.

Rose decided they all needed a change of pace.

"Lets all go in and relax in the living room while Carla prepares some dinner for us. I'm having her make her specialty, hamburgers and homemade French fries." They all followed her into the other room. It seemed as if Annie and Jimmy were in some kind of a trance as they took a seat near one another.

Upstairs, Skyler slept on with the two little dogs at her feet. She snuggled in deeply with her favorite pillow cradling her sweet little blonde head. This nap was full of sugar plum fairies and white unicorns and she dreamed the things all children are supposed to. She smiled while she slept, feeling warm, safe, and loved.

Downstairs, her parents were in transition. For Jimmy, he was feeling like a dad for the first time, and he wanted to protect Skyler. He was deeply ashamed of the thirty-six year old man he'd become. Looking over at his sixteen-year-old son, it hit him that he had no right to be called 'Dad.' He'd never done anything to deserve that title.

He'd made a choice to do drugs instead of taking care of his family. It almost ruined his life, almost, but not completely. He was getting another chance thanks to Rose. He owed her so much already, but this, this invitation to stay here with his kids, was a miracle. It humbled him like nothing else in his life ever had.

Annie kept looking at Jimmy's hands. She remembered him holding Bo when he was a tiny baby. There were a lot of good times back then, more good than bad. She'd really messed up. She had failed them all. It had taken Skyler to be kidnapped, and her own abduction for her to realize what her family meant to her.

She took a drink of her cocoa and asked her mother if she had room for her there as well. "I don't really have any roots in the city, Mom. The apartment is leased, so I can get out of that pretty easy. I see now that I was running away from raising the kids alone. I think I was petrified of messing up. Do you think I can have my old room back?"

When Annie was recovering from her own ordeal, she had ended all ties with people who were in her life. She had walked away from it all the day she came back home and spent time with Skyler out in the gazebo. She knew that her life was about to change.

This day had been a day of miracles. Rose opened up her arms, and Annie went into them. She held her a moment, before speaking.

"I love you, Annie. Welcome home. Tomorrow we got an appointment with God. All four of you are going to be in the front row. We have experienced many blessings and even miracles, and there's going to be some praise." She had tears full of gratitude swimming in her eyes. Rose hugged her daughter.

"Do you have any objections sweetheart?" she asked. Annie shook her head.

"What time does the bus leave?" she asked her mother.

"7 AM sharp. Now, excuse me, I have a sermon to write. See you all at six, for dinner." She embraced them all before turning to walk upstairs.

Bo turned to Jimmy, looking his dad up and down.

"You know Dad, I think I got a few shirts you can try on. What do you think?" Jimmy grinned at him and ruffled his hair.

"Good idea, Son. Good idea." He winked at Annie.

"See you at dinner in a while." After reaching out and gently touching her hand, he followed Bo upstairs and disappeared around the corner.

Annie stood alone downstairs, suddenly feeling a pull to go up and check on Skyler. She just wanted to see her there, tucked into her bed. She felt like a stranger here, yet she knew it was where she was supposed to be.

Home was a place she'd left so many years ago, and now everything was different, yet nothing here had changed. She was feeling something strange, a peaceful feeling. She wanted to put her finger on it, to define it. As she stood looking at her daughters sleeping form, she realized what the foreign feeling was. It was contentment. Her family was safe and she was home.

9

Revelation

The walls were dancing with light from the candles, lit at intervals down the ivory colored panels. A very special ambiance was being created with the harmonious chords of the pipe organ. Throngs of people were filing in.

The church had been built to hold three hundred people, and it seemed that there were almost exactly that, as the faces were shoulder to shoulder. The men, women, and children all chattered quietly and fidgeted, as they waited for the Reverend Rose England to appear.

Annie had never been here before, and neither had Jimmy. Bo and Skyler stood between the two, protecting them, connecting them. A lot of the congregation had figured out who they were, and as they stared at the back of Annie's head, she had a sudden urge to flee.

As the service started, there was a thundering and swelling of music. A choir sang out their praises. Then a lector read a reading taken from Isaiah 35. The verse spoke about the return of the redeemed to Zion.

Rose stepped up to the podium, and asked her audience to be seated. She greeted them.

"Good morning church family."

They responded back, "Good morning Pastor Rose." She smiled at the crowd before her, and launched into her sermon.

"Today I'm going to tell you a story. It is about miracles and roads that lead back home. It all began thirty-six years ago, when the doctors told me, I would never conceive." I accepted that, and went on, never expecting a child. I got a dog instead."

At this statement, several snickers could be heard through the crowd.

"I was twenty-one when I found out I was pregnant. Unwed and living alone, I was trying to go to school in the evening to get an Associates Degree in Accounting. When the doctor gave me the news, I was not sure what to think. Nine months later, my daughter Annie was born. She has held my heart ever since. She is right here today in the front row."

Rose smiled down at Annie from the podium and Annie turned several shades of red, as the entire congregation focused on her.

"I got my degree, but accounting was boring. I needed to connect with people, so I got a job at Denny's as a waitress. Something was driving me towards the ministry, I never did figure out what, maybe it was the hungry, homeless people I saw.

Sometimes I felt like scraping a plate full of food into a brown bag, and discreetly laying it on the seat beside them, because I saw they were reluctant to leave the booth. It seemed to me they were not sure when they would get another meal. I did wrap up a sandwich a few times, just to see a smile.

A few years later, when Annie was about four, I put her in preschool and got myself into the seminary. You see, through serving folks food, I had seen another hunger. It was spiritual. They were so lost sometimes, crying and telling me stories of heartache and brokenness. With my Ordination, I was able to answer a call to help.

Faith was my answer to every problem. Faith that somehow through whatever life throws at you, you will rise up and throw it back. Faith that no matter how long it takes, if you continue to believe that all roads lead back to home, then you'll find your way there.

Folks, my daughter Annie's here today, with her children and their father, Jimmy.

The road has taken them around some very sharp curves, and even thrown them off of some dangerous deadly cliffs. They floundered in the dark for a path to take them back up, but it was as if they were wondering blindly, because they were.

It has been eight years since they have sat together on a bench.

So today I want to make a conscious acknowledgement that they have finally found the right path. They have made it home."

Rose's voice had picked up a quiver. She stopped a moment, looked down at her notes and gathered her emotions to continue.

"We have faced some horrific events in the past three weeks. I would like to compare it to people swimming toward shore after almost drowning. They can see the shore, and are thrashing wildly to reach it, but something dark and deep keeps pulling them under. There is a fight going on with the tides and undertows. The opponent is a powerful force that wants to drown them, but on the shore they can see their children waiting, beckoning, needing them to be strong.

Today you are witnessing something miraculous. The four people sitting here today in the front row are my family, and I'm going to ask them to stand up, as we congratulate them on making it to the shore. Welcome home."

Jimmy and Annie were crying, and as they each grabbed their children's hands, they all stood. Rose started applauding, and everyone joined her. There were shouts of, 'Amen', and 'Praise God'. The room was filled with noise that seemed to bounce around and straight into the hearts of the four standing. It went on for a full minute.

Finally as the church grew quiet, and everyone sat and stilled, a lector stepped to the microphone.

"We will now share a reading from Jeremiah 31: verses 16-17."

"Thus says the lord: Keep your voices from weeping, and your eyes from tears; for there is a reward for your work, says the Lord: they shall come back from the land of the enemy; there is hope for your future, says the Lord: your children shall come back to their own country.

Now, hear what the Spirit is saying to the Church."

As the lector sat down, the music rose again. It was a song called "The River." Rose reflected on the song, and was reminded that the name of her church was Rivers Oak. The oak tree takes root, and years and years later it becomes a great giant of a tree. She knew that her church would be like that tree.

She again took her place in front of the microphone. There was complete quiet now as she spoke.

"Please join me as we pray and give thanks to God for all of our blessings."

"Father, we thank You for every road that leads back home. We thank You for giving us light on our darkest path. We ask that You keep us safe from the dark forces that lead us away from the light of Your love. Thank You for bringing everyone here today to hear a message of hope. No matter how many years we wander in darkness, there is always a light that we can see if we just look up. It leads us to a place where we are unconditionally loved and accepted. We ask that You continue to embrace the brokenness that we hold in our hearts, and rock us as we are held in Your lap Father. We ask all of this and we thank You Father. In Jesus' name, Amen."

Rose nodded her head to the musicians seated in the rear of the pulpit, and took a seat. All around them rose glorious sound as the singers took the microphones over, and heavenly voices sang praise.

Jimmy could not speak. As the service ended, and the congregation filed out of their seats, they did not go toward the door. Instead they flowed toward Jimmy, Annie, Bo, and Skyler. The family was welcomed and blessed, as they were embraced by Rose's church family. She just sat there watching…grateful. It was a day she would never forget.

The ride home was different than the ride to church. They felt loved and happy together in the tight space. There was a strand of love sewn into their collective souls at church today, bonding them.

Five people that had not been together a year ago could never imagine being separated now.

As the gates to the compound opened up, they entered into sacred safety. Carla let the little dogs out to run and greet the family. Bo and Skyler embarked and stood laughing with glee, as the two dogs ran around and around their feet. It was a noise that bounced into every crevice of the hills and valleys. It was a noise that reached the skies and echoed up to Heaven.

The next day, as discussed, Rose accompanied by Jimmy and Annie, took Skyler down to the Police Station to make a complete statement. Being a minor child, she would not be asked to be present at the trial of Samuels and Banks. They would use a videotaped interview.

She was nervous. There were so many people in the room, milling about. A man in a suit and tie came over and started explaining what would happen.

"Skyler, my name is Philip Bailey, I'm a detective with the precinct. You will be asked to swear on a Bible that you will tell the truth. Do you understand that? You must tell the truth, it's the most important thing."

"Yes, I understood." Then, she asked them something they thought was highly unusual. She asked them if she could make a special tape, to speak to her captor, Terry Samuels.

The detective in charge of gathering her statement was taken aback by the request. He told her it was up to her Parents. Rose asked Skyler why she wanted to speak to her kidnapper.

"He set me free, Grandma. He showed me pictures of his kids, and we ate pizza together. He got me extra cheese. I feel connected to him somehow. I want to wish him well, and tell him thank you. Is it okay?"

Rose didn't see any harm in it. If it was what Skyler wanted, then it was okay with her.

After an hour and ten minutes, everything they needed to be presented in court was recorded. She was officially finished, and they thanked her. Skyler took a break to get something to drink, and think about what she wanted to say to Terry Samuels. Then, she went back into the room. Her dad, mom and grandma were all there, waiting for her. They told her, she needed to keep her comments brief.

Once again, Detective Bailey set her up near the microphone. She was told to speak up, the tape was rolling; she could talk whenever she was ready. Skyler looked at the camera and spoke to Terry Samuels.

"I just wanted to say thanks, Mister. Thanks for being nice and for letting me go home. I hope you can get out someday, and go see your kids. My grandma always says that you can be forgiven for anything, if you just believe that Jesus died for your sins. I forgive you for taking me. Don't lose hope of getting out someday. Good luck, Mister. That's all I wanted to say. Good bye."

The detective grinned. He told her it was a wrap, and he would make sure it was given to the accused. As Skyler and her family left the room, he just shook his head. He was thinking she was an unusual child.

There was another important appointment today with Dr. Matthew Roads. First they headed out for lunch at Denny's, the very place where Rose had been a waitress over thirty-five years ago. It had all changed now, and so had she. The Lord had given her a life full of surprises and blessings, three of which were seated in front of her now, playing spitball with their straws.

They were ushered into Matthew's office an hour later. Jimmy and Annie sat on either side of Skyler. Rose took a chair across the room. After introductions, the recorder was switched on and as things got quiet; all four listened to the clock on the wall, ticking.

The dynamic was different this time for Matthew. As he observed her, she seemed to stand out among the others. She was a glowing blonde child with healthy pink cheeks. Her eyes held him as he asked her to describe how she felt today.

Skyler talked to him for a full twenty minutes without stopping.

"I was sleeping in a chair. There was a bright light behind my eyes like a million diamonds and I woke up." She told them she didn't understand why.

It was a good thing he was recording, because he could not digest it all immediately. As she spoke, he took continuous tiny notes on his legal pad. This case was astonishing. She was extraordinary.

Finally she stopped, and as she paused, they all squirmed in their seats, uncomfortable somehow with what they were being asked to accept. She looked at all of their faces, and the reactions they revealed. Her mother's showed worry, while her dad's showed confusion. She understood, it was all so unbelievable, but it was true.

"I guess that's it. I just wish no little kids had to get shot at all. That would have been way better."

"I have a question, Doc," Jimmy spoke up. "Why does she only see things while she's asleep?"

Matthew smiled at him.

"This has got to be incredibly difficult for you and Ms. England to swallow. The only thing I can tell you is this: I've seen many kinds of phenomena like this, but hers is unique. I'll answer more questions in a moment. First, I'd like to share some details from a special young man's case with you.

"The case was reported and brought before me two years ago. He was fourteen years old and one of the only documented cases that have been confirmed of premonitions here in Missouri. There are a few slight similarities to Skylers case. I'm not at liberty to say his name, so I'll just refer to him as Joe. When he first came to see me, it was because he was seeing things happen, before they happened.

"One of his very first premonitions was of a car accident. He was actually on the school bus reading when he heard a crash, and looked out the window.

"He said there was nothing there, but a few minutes later, something happened. A car in an intersection nearby hit another car. As the bus continued on, Joe was shaking his head, wondering why he saw it before it happened.

"Other incidents happened at unusual intervals, mostly during wakeful times. Another example I will share is one that involved his sister.

"His parents were out of town and she and Joe were watching a program on television. Joe suddenly got up and locked the door. He told his sister that there was danger, and they went around the house locking the windows and making sure the drapes were closed. Before they went upstairs that night, Joe put a heavy desk in front of the front door.

"That night, there was an attempted home invasion. Someone was trying to kick the door in, but Joe turned the outside lights on, and the intruder ran away. He called police, and was unable to explain to them that he'd actually prevented it because he had experienced a premonition. He simply left that information out.

"It was after a few more incidents that we finally met Joe. He was scheduled for a complete examination. We were able to identify unusual brain waves in his physical work up. Most people have comparable brain waves, but Joe's brain waves showed deeper continuous shades on the scans.

"An example would be if you were thinking about eating a sandwich. It would be a casual thought that would be light blue on a brain scan. For Joe, all of his casual thoughts were in deeper shades. They were extremely consistent, where normal activity will fluctuate. If we are relaxed for example, and listening to soft music, our brain waves can be almost transparent. For Joe, his brain waves never stopped their bold continuous flow. Even in states of complete relaxation, the activity levels were as if he were running.

"I have scheduled a special test for Skyler next Monday, if that's okay." He glanced at Skyler, then around to the others.

"We will require a consent form and she will also be required to spend the night. Her circumstances are different than Joe's. Skyler is sleeping when she experiences the psychic visions.

"From here on out, I will also have a few of my comrades observing diagnostic examinations. I am excited to explore what's happening to Skyler. Now, Mr. Conrad, I will be happy to answer any questions you have."

"Is there anything we can do to keep her from seeing bad things Doc?" Jimmy was first to inquire.

"I understand you want to protect her, but these are things of the mind. There is nothing we can do to keep her brain from seeing what it is going to see. We would never sanction drugs, or hypnosis to curtail what is happening with her. Documentation and therapy to help her understand and get through the unexplainable parts of these visions, is all we can offer. The rest is up to God."

The four of them sat a moment, digesting what the doctor had just said.

Then Annie spoke up, "Dr. Roads, I'm so frightened that somehow she will be damaged from seeing these things. She is watching some kind of horror films in these premonitions. I mean, she saw a child get shot a few days ago." Annie grabbed Skyler's hand, reassuring her.

Matthew studied Annie, trying to find words to comfort her.

"I don't believe any harm can come to her. We can't shield her in any way from what she sees happen. We can just reassure her it's a vision. I wish I had an explanation for this. The fact is, just as certain people have amazing artistic or musical ability, she has unusual psychic ability. She is unique and special." Matthew was smiling toward Skyler. He winked.

Rose spoke up then, "Do you think it's temporary Matthew? Do you think she could grow out of it?"

"That's possible Rose. We're all just guessing why, when or how. I can't answer those questions."

Matthew came around holding his hand out to Jimmy, then Annie.

"It was real nice to meet you folks. Your little girl will be safe with us."

"I'm worried about publicity Matthew." Rose needed reassurance.

"Can you give us your word that you can keep it all confidential as we move forward with more analysis of her condition? I would like to keep this just within the family."

"We will do everything in our power, Rose. Sometimes, these things do get leaked out. For example, the young man we spoke of before: we were able to seal his records, but as the family spoke about it, and asked for prayer in the community, word spread about his abilities. Sometimes, it just gets out."

They all told him, "Thank you," and the following Monday was set on the calendar for her overnight analysis.

Meanwhile, Rose was highly worried about the press as the newspapers printed a story about Skylers kidnapping, and the phone rang daily for consent to interview the family. Rose consistently declined.

One week had gone by since they'd gone to the movies and Skyler was taken. Things were quiet at the house. The kids were back in school and Jimmy and Annie took turns with Carla to pick them up.

Monday rolled in uneventfully, and it was the day of her psychological work-up. It was decided Rose would be the guardian that stayed with her. Skyler packed a small bag with her toothbrush, favorite nightgown, robe, and slippers. She kissed both dogs goodbye and told them not to worry. She whispered her affection and assured them she would be home the next day.

The family hugged her, and waved as the Mercedes left the compound. The destination was Chesterfield, where the Mayo Clinic of St. Louis was located. There would be a room set up for Rose, just beyond where Sky would be sleeping.

It was 7 PM, and Skyler was being hooked up with several feeds that were attached to three different screens. One was simply recording brain waves, one breathing and heart rate, and the other was recording nerve impulses.

She was listening to an audio book through the earpiece. It was designed to allow her to slowly enter sleep REM's. She seemed relaxed and normal. As Dr. Roads and two of his colleagues quietly monitored the devices, nothing was amiss.

A few hours later, Rose, who'd been reading her Sunday sermon plan for the month, was falling asleep as well. She yawned, pulled the blanket up around her, and found the cushy part of the cot. After about thirteen minutes, she was gently snoring.

The audience watching Skyler's monitors as she slept took turns napping on a couch in the observation room. Three-hour intervals were allowed for renewed alertness. There were two men watching the screens at all times through the night. The objective was to conclude the study at 6 AM and awaken their subject.

It was 4:45AM, when the steady repetitive pattern on the brainwave screen started to become erratic. The observation room awoke, and everyone gathered together, watching the screens. Sky was experiencing something in her deepest sleep state that was causing the screens to change.

Suddenly Skyler woke up, and all of the equipment came alive with activity. She started speaking, "Grandma. Grandma!"

Her eyes came wide open as she lifted her head and looked at the glass window. Matthew threw down his headpiece and entered the room. At the very same moment, Rose heard Skyler calling her, and woke up. She flung the covers off, and ran into the next room.

All three technicians were unhooking Skyler so she could be embraced by her grandmother. Rose sat on the bed, lifted her sweet little granddaughter into her arms, and put her head on her shoulder.

"What is it Sky? What's the matter?" She started rocking her.

Skyler was wide-awake now, and she was shaking.

"We have to call home right away. It's a big brown snake, and it's going to kill Martin. Call Bo, and tell him it's under the bush, by the back patio. It's going to get Martin!"

Rose reassured her, saying she would call right away, and it was going to be fine. She looked at Matthew, and shook her head. The poor baby was very distraught. Rose held her tightly; crooning to her that it was all right. She felt helpless to do anything to make her feel better.

Matthew was sure there was a snake in the backyard. Martin was one of the family's Chihuahuas and he knew a venomous bite could definitely kill the tiny dog.

Rose asked them if she could just lay with Skyler now and reassure her. The vision of the snake fangs going into the beloved pup's body had left her highly disturbed.

Matthew told Rose they had everything recorded, and it was going to be enough. Skyler's brain waves would tell them a very interesting story.

At 5 AM, Rose made the call. Carla answered in her usual manner, her Spanish dialect strong this morning, "England residence."

Rose said, "Carla, Skyler has had a vision out here."

"Jdios mio, otra vez!" Carla exclaimed.

"Yes, it is pretty scary. She woke us up to tell us a snake was in the yard. I need you to go tell everyone in the house that Skyler has seen a venomous snake under the bush by the backdoor. It's on the right side of the patio. She saw Martin getting bit!"

Carla said, "Si, Senorita England, I will go tell everyone, and we will have someone come right away!"

"Yes Carla, do it now. Gracias." Rose hung up the phone, and went back to Skyler's side, reassuring her softly, "Just rest now sweet, everything's going to be fine. Nothing's going to hurt the puppies."

Matthew concluded the morning with a hug for Skyler. He told her she was just an amazingly gifted child, and he would call them all in when he reached some conclusions about the data they had gathered. After shaking Rose's hand, he asked her to call him when they found out details about the snake. He wanted to document everything into her record. Then he turned to join his comrades in the other room, conferring with them quietly.

As Rose passed the glass, she looked into the room. The three men seemed consumed with the equipment, and were writing extensively on a legal pad, oblivious to the fact that Rose was watching their expressions. It hit her that to them, Skyler was some kind of experiment. That disturbed her, but even more disturbing was the realization that a snake could have bitten and killed one of the dogs. They were in for some sleepless nights if these visions increased.

As Skyler dressed for the way home, she was tired. The vision had scared her badly this time. The snake wasn't big, but she knew it could be deadly. She was anxious to get home, and see for herself that everything was fine.

Bo had gone outside first, then Jimmy. Five minutes later Annie came rambling out as well, with Carla shadowing her, staying back. The two dogs were still upstairs in Skyler's bed, but they would need to be let out very soon. Bo went to the shed and got two tools: a garden rake and a hoe. He handed the hoe to Jimmy.

"Dad, I'm going to push the bush a little, and if you see the snake move, kill it."

Jimmy paled a little, and nodded his head. Annie and Carla were at least fifteen feet away. Jimmy raised the sharp tool up; ready to strike as Bo gingerly pulled the bush away with the rake.

Annie said, "Be careful Bo, I don't want you bitten."

"It's okay, Mom. Relax, we got this."

On the third push with the rake, suddenly the snake was revealed, brown and slithering away, heading toward the foundation of the house. Jimmy lunged forward and stabbed it with the hoe. The snake kept moving, and Jimmy chopped at its neck, cutting the head almost entirely off of the snake's body.

Annie started screaming, "Oh my Gosh! Oh my Gosh!" Carla turned tail and ran in the house. She had a case of the heebie jeebies.

Jimmy looked at Bo and said, "I think we got it, Son. Good job." The two went in for high fives and stood staring at the snake.

"I think it's a copperhead, Dad. Look at the diamond pattern and the way its head is shaped. I'm pretty sure it is."

They left it there a moment, and went inside to look it up on the computer. Sure enough, it was a copperhead. If it had bitten Martin, he would have most assuredly died from it.

The two trekked back out and made a large hole in the back of the shed to bury the snake, finally, they let the two little dogs out to run the yard.

Bo called his grandmother. It was 6:30 AM and she was on her way home with Skyler. She felt such relief when she heard they had killed the snake and buried it.

Rose told Skyler the news. She laid her head back on the seat and said. "Grandma, if I didn't have these visions, Martin or Matilda could have died from that snake. I guess it's kind of good, but that was just so scary. I hope I never really do see a bad snake like that again, unless it's behind the glass in a real zoo."

Later, as they arrived home, Bo and Jimmy told them all of the details. Rose listened, shaking her head. "Thank God Skyler saw it. I just can't believe it, I have to call Matthew."

"It was a copperhead Matthew, quite large actually. The boys killed it and buried it out behind our shed. Yes, I know, we talked about that. She is grateful she had the vision. Okay, we'll talk soon. Okay, I'll tell her. Thank you, good-bye."

It was nice to be home. Skyler was tired, and as she lay down on the sofa, both dogs jumped right up, joining her. They knew she had not been home last night, and they were completely happy to stay beside her now. Matilda went up closer and laid her little head on her mistress' neck, looking at her adoringly. Skyler rubbed both of their heads.

"Martin, if only you knew how dangerous it would have been for you outside this morning, and you too, Tildy." She was chatting quietly to her little audience. They both raised their eyebrows making tiny noises as if answering.

Annie came over and put a big blanket on Sky and sat down next to her to channel surf. They decided to watch *"Cinderella"* but, within ten minutes, Annie knew she was watching it alone. She wasn't really listening to the movie; she was listening to something else. She was listening to Skyler breathing as she slept peacefully.

Annie touched her daughter's silky hair, moving even closer to her. She wanted to feel her heartbeat. She took Skyler's small hand in hers and gently held it, connecting herself with her baby girl.

A short while later, Jimmy and Bo came in to the room. Both of them stood staring at the scene. It was so sweet. They quietly tiptoed out, feeling all mushy inside. It made them happy.

"Hey Bo, I have an idea." Jimmy turned to his boy, as they traversed the house heading for the kitchen.

"What's that, Dad?"

"Let's go for a drive. Go ask Rose for the keys to the Corvette. I'm going to see if you can drive a real car."

"Really?" Bo felt himself getting excited. "Okay, be right back." He flew across the house and slid up to Rose's door. He knocked quietly.

"Come in,"

"Hi, Grandma, are you doing okay?" She was lying there on top of the covers with the afghan wrapped all around her, watching Joyce Meyer on the television.

"Oh yes, Sweetheart, just a little worn out from all of the excitement. Are you okay?"

"Yea. Hey listen: Dad wants to know if we can take the Corvette out for a spin? Please? I mean, if you don't mind. I sure would like a chance to drive it now that I have my learner's permit." He was grinning and she was enjoying that very much.

"Yes. You guys just be careful and fill it up for me if you don't mind." She held her arms out to Bo, and he went into them.

"Don't you ding that car, Bo. It's in pristine condition."

"Oh, I'll be careful, I promise. Thanks Grandma, you are the best. Woo Hoo!" Bo turned and headed out.

Rose asked him to tell Carla she could use a cup of tea. He said, "No problem," and then, "I love you Grandma." She listened as he tore down the stairs.

"I love you more," she hollered after him, and continued grinning long after he left her room.

10
Robbery

There was a feeling of calm over the compound. As summer was being ushered in, they had gone months with silent nights.

The analyses of Skyler's tests were conclusive. She had extraordinarily active brain waves, similar to her counterpart study subject, Joe.

Dr. Roads had written it all down, but there was nothing else to be done. She had psychic abilities that were beyond anything ever reported. The possibility of them growing even stronger intrigued him, since she was so young.

Skyler would be turning eleven on July twenty-eighth, and Rose was planning a celebration. The kids were allowed to invite a few of their friends over. Rose invited a few close friends from church, and they were having it catered. There would be some old fashioned games outside, like croquet, and Bob the Apple. Rose had even set up a Pin the Tail on the Donkey game, which was an old family favorite.

Jimmy and Annie were making cupcakes for their daughter, in the shape of a dog, or at least that was their plan. They laid it all out ahead of time, laughing and teasing one another.

Rose watched from afar as they seemed to be bonding all over again. She had said many prayers for them, praying they would see the gift of being parents to such fine sweet children as Skyler and Bo.

The gates to the compound were opened, and as the folks arrived there was a feeling of celebration. Rose was thoroughly enjoying having her family stay with her. She couldn't ask for anything more than what she had these days.

There was going to be a special surprise for Skyler. Rose had arranged to have several large fireworks set up in the backfield to be shot off as soon as it got dark. Skyler loved fireworks, and Rose could barely contain her excitement and anticipation of the event.

At dusk, she started rounding up everyone and told him or her to go to the backyard for a surprise. People slowly trickled back until finally all were assembled.

Rose took a spot in front of the crowd, addressing them.

"I wanted to wish you a very special eleventh birthday, Skyler Marie Conrad, we love you."

All of a sudden they heard deep booms and the sky was lit up with the most beautiful fireworks display. Eighteen faces were turned up to the sky…and it was magical. Rose had spent $700 for the bright bursts of color. To see the look on her baby girl's face was worth every penny.

As the party was winding down and people started to trickle out of the compound, Skyler sidled up to her grandmother and asked if her friend June could stay over. It was summer after all.

Rose told her that it would be fine as long as her folks were okay with it. June called her mom and permission was granted. The two girls ran upstairs to watch a concert. They were in love with some boys in the band. It was such typical pre-teen behavior, and that normalcy in itself was an answer to prayer.

They were all thrilled Skyler had a special friend. After helping Carla get everything cleaned up and put away, they stayed up late playing cards and talking about how much everyone enjoyed themselves. This was the first real party Rose ever hosted. She was thinking they needed to do it more often.

The contented calm of the warm summer night was to be short lived. Skyler came into Rose's room at four AM and got into bed with her. She gently shook her grandmother awake. She was crying and her voice was shaking.

"Grandma, something real bad is going to happen." Rose sat up immediately, asking Skyler what she'd seen.

"I saw a bad man and he's going into June's house. Her mom and dad are sleeping and he's going upstairs. He's going into their room and he has a gun."

"Oh my God, Skyler!" Rose jumped up and grabbed the phone. She called 9 11 and told them who she was, and that she had reason to believe a robbery was in progress. They asked her how she knew and she told them she had just been given a tip.

After giving them the address of June's home, she and Skyler went into the living room. She was being very careful not to awaken the household as she consoled her granddaughter. Fifteen minutes later, there was a buzz from the gate. The police wanted to talk to her. Rose buzzed the gate, and it opened.

She was in the foyer as they knocked. She let them in. Skyler stood there as well, silently. She was so tired and wished she could go back up to bed. These visions were so scary and she was very tired of waking up with the violent images.

"Ms. Rose England?" the one on the left asked her.

"Yes, that's me," she told them.

"Ms. England, I'm Officer Nick Hodges and this is my partner Tyler Alan. Can we sit down for a minute? There are a few things we need to clear up." Rose waved them into the living room. Both officers followed, and sat on the sofa facing her. Skyler sat on the arm of the chair very close to her grandmother.

Annie had come downstairs. Her bedroom was facing the front of the large house and she heard the car slowly moving up the gravel drive. She hesitantly entered the room, her heartbeat quickened when she saw the police sitting on the sofa.

"What's going on, Mom?" she asked.

"Oh Annie, Skyler has had a vision." The officers looked from Rose to Skyler, and then Annie with confused expressions.

"Come and sit down, I might need help explaining things to them."

Officer Hodges started talking.

"We need to clear up some confusion, Ms. England. The call came in at 4:08 AM that a robbery was in progress. We went to the address, but there were no problems. Upon further inspection of the immediate vicinity, we noticed a suspicious vehicle parked on the curb. At that time, we apprehended a young man just as he was coming from behind a house. He had several items in his possession that we believe he'd taken from a residence down the road. We also found a 45 pistol on his person.

"We believe he robbed several residences on this street, the question is…how did you know this individual was in that area, Ms. England?"

"Officer Hodges," Rose began, trying to find the words. She gently grabbed Skylers hand and brought her to her lap.

"This is my granddaughter Skyler Conrad. I think you may have heard of the kidnapping a few months ago?" Rose waited for them to acknowledge they remembered. A light seemed to come on in their eyes as they both nodded.

"It was Skyler that was taken. I can't really explain why she was released, but it had to do with something she saw in her dream. Oh my goodness, this is just too confusing to explain." Rose took a breath, looking toward Annie.

"You're doing fine, Mom, keep going."

Rose nodded and continued, "Skyler has some kind of unusual psychic warning system. We do not understand it, but she sees visions while she's asleep and when she wakes, she is able to warn us."

Officer Nick Hodges had never heard anything like this. He looked at his partner, Tyler, who was sitting there with his mouth open. Neither one of them understand what she was saying.

Rose continued explaining, "So, the visions always wake her up. She came into my room this morning telling me she had seen a bad man at her friend June's house. The man she saw was in the home and had a gun. She felt he was there to rob the folks at 1406 Peyton Drive. There's more, their little girl June is upstairs sleeping. She's Skyler's friend. You see, usually when Skyler sees something it involves someone she knows. It usually involves danger and some evil deed. In this case, the man in her dream had a gun."

This was getting more bizarre by the second. Tyler and Nick just sat there a minute, thinking this lady and her granddaughter had a few screws lose. Then Annie started to speak.

"My name is Annie Mae England, I'm Skyler's mom. Five months ago, some really bad guys took me from a club in Illinois. They were involved in human trafficking and I was targeted to be their next investment. Skyler saw it, but what she saw hadn't happened yet. In her vision, I was already unconscious and being carried to the river. She saved me. The police came just in time. If not for her they would've found me dead, in the river."

"I think I remember that incident vaguely." Officer Hodges was looking at her. "I have a confession Ms. England, I've actually seen you perform at the Pink Cabaret at my brother-in-laws bachelor party." He was smiling at her and blushing slightly.

"I guess I didn't really need to volunteer that information, but I do remember the case, because I remember you."

Officer Alan spoke up, "So let me get this straight. You are telling us that Skyler here, saw you getting abducted and she alerted police?" He was looking from Annie, to Skyler, and then to Rose.

"Yes, that's exactly what I'm saying. It's a miracle she saw something that hadn't happened yet. In her vision, they were going to kill me and throw me in the river!" Annie's voice was breaking up now, as she remembered the miraculous events. It still just floored her that Skyler had saved her life.

About this time, Jimmy came downstairs. He thought he heard a television on somewhere in the house, but now he realized something was happening.

"Anne?" he asked. "What's going on? Skyler? Are you okay, Sweetheart?"

Skyler nodded and told him, "I had a vision, Daddy. It was at June's mommy and daddy's house, and a bad man was going up the stairs where they were sleeping."

Jimmy put his hands to his head and started rubbing them over his eyes. "Oh my God! I'm sorry Sweetheart; did it scare you?"

"Yes, it was very scary! I told Grandma and she called the police and they caught him."

This was all just too much to take in. The two officers looked from Jimmy, to Annie, to Rose and then at the little blonde child who was standing in front of them talking about visions. They decided to table it for now.

"Listen folks, can you come down to the station later this afternoon? I would say after lunch would be good for us. We're going to need statements and we have to get some advice about how to proceed. For now, if Skyler averted a robbery somehow, then it's a good thing. We're heading out, folks. Talk to you again tomorrow, okay?" Officer Alan handed them a card. "Give us a call if you have any questions."

"Okay," Rose said, and followed them to the door. "We'll be there around 1 PM. Good-bye and thanks."

Jimmy shook both officers hands and told them, "Thanks."

Annie just nodded at them both, and shut the door.

Jimmy wanted to hear more. He had a question on his face and concern in his eyes.

"They caught the man? Wow, that's just unbelievable. I'm going to make some coffee, then you need to tell me more Pumpkin." Shaking his head, he went into the kitchen.

As he went about the task, Rose sat at the breakfast bar, Skyler and Annie followed suit.

"I guess another horrible deed was stopped. The Lord has been using you in such a miraculous way, Sweetheart. I wish I could protect you from this but I have no power over it. It's supernatural."

"I know, Grandma. I'm not sure why I'm the one who He decided to give this to. I'm glad you're here with me though, at least I know you'll help me understand it."

Skyler looked at her mom and dad adding, "I'm glad you're both here too. I feel like a circle is around me, and it makes me feel better. I think I'm going to go back upstairs now, and go back to sleep." She yawned.

"Good idea, Sweetie," Annie said. "We'll see you in a few hours at breakfast. Try and get some rest." She put her arms around Skyler, hugged her and kissed the top of her sweet blonde head.

Two hours later, Bo wandered down the stairs. His dad was on the sofa snoozing, with Cleo the cat snuggled up on his chest. Andy Griffith played quietly on the television.

"What's up, Daddy-o?" he asked, reaching over to scratch Cleo's head.

"You aren't going to believe it, Bo." Jimmy sat up, took a sip of his tepid coffee, and grimaced. "Let me get something going for breakfast while I tell you all about it."

About that time, Martin started crying at the door, so Bo let him out. He had a perplexed expression on his face as he turned back to his dad, who was gathering eggs and sausage out of the fridge.

Jimmy started telling his son what happened in the wee hours of the morning. "Your sister had a vision at 4 AM. She saw an attempted robbery and the man had a gun. It was her friend June's house and in Sky's vision, the parents were upstairs sleeping and the man was coming into their room. Grandma called the police and they were here. Meanwhile, they caught a guy and he was definitely the one Sky saw. He had a gun and he had just finished robbing a house two doors down."

Bo just stood there completely bewildered. "I don't believe that. I mean, I do, but wow, I'm so amazed."

"I know it's hard to fathom, Son. Rose, your mom and I are going down to the station with Skyler at 1 PM this afternoon. We have to do some explaining and I'm not sure how the police department is going to take the information about psychic visions. That's what worries me."

"I hear you, Dad. She's just a little girl. It's some kind of phenomena that we can't explain. I have to go to work at the store today, or else I'd go too." Bo offered.

"It's okay, Son, don't worry about it. We'll be with her and if we have to, we can call Dr. Roads down to the station to help explain the psychic part of what's happening. I just hate to see it go public, that scares me."

Jimmy continued making breakfast, while quietly sharing his concerns with his son. The two had formed a bond these past six months, while Jimmy taught Bo how to drive.

It was after 9 AM, when Skyler and her friend June appeared at the kitchen table.

"Hungry, girls?" Jimmy asked from in the other room.

"Yes Daddy, can we have some pancakes?" Skyler smiled at her friend.

"My Dad makes really good pancakes. Want some?"

"Sounds delicious. Do you have any orange juice?" June asked her new best friend.

"Oh yea, we got all kinds of juice." Skyler was looking for Bo this morning.

"Did you see Bo this morning, Dad?" she asked Jimmy.

"Yea sweetheart, he had to go to work. Carla drove him in a few minutes ago." He was watching her face.

"Okay, I guess I'll see him later." Skyler turned to her brother when things upset her. She was trying not to think about what had happened this morning, but she felt like she needed Bo. It would have to wait.

Carla came in soon after and informed June that her parents had called to say they would come pick her up at eleven. She nodded her head and said, "Thanks Carla."

Rose came into the kitchen, sniffing. "I smell food. Jimmy, have you got any extra? That smells amazing."

"Sure thing," Jimmy said. "Sausage, eggs and pancakes coming right up."

Rose turned to Carla and said, "Carla, can I see you a minute in my office?" Carla nodded, following her down the hall.

"Something happened this morning. While you were snug in your bed sleeping, Skyler had a vision. Oh Carla, the poor thing saw her friend's folks getting robbed. I called the police and they caught him. The police were here at 5 AM this morning. It was so confusing. We have to go down and talk to them again this afternoon."

Carla said, "Jesu' poor nina."

Rose said, "Yes, poor baby, she's gone through so much. I'm not sure what's going to happen today Carla, but to go on record with all of this is so scary. You know it could go public now. We've been lucky so far that we could keep it within the family."

"No worries, Ms. Rosa. The Lord will watch over our nina. We will put it in his hands, Si?"

"You are right Carla, we'll trust Him." Rose took hold of Carla's hands and closed her eyes, praying quietly that God would help them to explain and except this supernatural gift. When Rose was finished, they both said, "Amen" in unison, and turned to join the others.

Rose felt better now as they headed for the kitchen. When they entered, the smell of food made their stomach's growl. Jimmy was cooking mounds of pancakes and sausage links. Annie and the girls were a rapt audience to his banter. One could never guess the extraordinary events of the early morning hours.

They all took a seat. Rose requested they join her in prayer. Then everyone got quiet as they started to consume the pancakes and sausage laid before them.

June really liked it here. Below her chair the little dogs were making tiny noises. She giggled a little, as Skyler tossed down a few scraps of sausage for them, smiling.

"Do you have any pets at your house, June?" Rose asked the girl.

"No, my mom is allergic to animal hair. We found that out when they got me a cat. Mommy got all itchy and broke out in a rash. It was sad, and I had to give the kitty away." June continued eating.

Annie said, "You can play with our cat Cleo anytime you want. It sure was a great party last night. I had so much fun. Did you have fun, Skyler?"

"Oh yes, Mom. Thanks for everything you guys did. It was the best birthday I've ever had." Between bites of sausage, she looked around the table. At that moment, she felt pretty lucky. Her family was together and she was a very happy little girl.

11

Puzzling Statements

The Chief of Police was standing against his desk, listening to a very confusing tale. Two of his best patrolmen, Alan and Hodges, were telling him a story about a tip that was phoned in and resulted in a successful arrest.

He wasn't used to a bunch of facts that didn't make sense. He told them to write it all down and put it on his desk. He would read it over and try to figure it out on his own. The main thing was, they caught a man in the act last night.

He would get answers as to why a little girl saw a robbery that had not actually happened. It was a puzzle, and he would have to lay the pieces out to put it together.

The family that called in the tip was coming in after lunch. He knew he'd get the crucial pieces he needed because he was going to be the one conducting the interview. He told his crew to alert him when the family arrived, went into his office, and shut the door.

Every police department had moles, and this one was no different. Her name was Rhonda Stiles, and she was the switchboard and 911 operator. She had records and recordings of every call that came in to the department. Her job included making sure it was all filed in such a way that a record could be produced immediately if it was needed.

She felt the press had a right to know about crime in the city. They called her at first for information and she was hesitant, but then it became a lucrative agreement. She was tapped into the local newspaper, receiving compensation for stories that checked out.

If she were caught leaking details from police reports, she'd be fired. She was careful to whom she talked to, and from where.

Rhonda was reading over the calls from last night. She found one tip on a robbery interesting. The tip involved a certain address, but the team had brought in a suspect that had robbed a house down the street. She shrugged it off, thinking there was obviously a mistake made on the house number itself.

Alan and Hodges passed by her desk.

"Hey, what are you two up to?" She called out to them.

Tyler slowed and stepped over to chat with her, Nick was right on his heels, grinning.

"How're you doing, Rhonda?" Tyler had asked her out a couple of times, but she always declined, declaring she didn't date cops.

"Oh, fine and dandy. What kind of call took you out to Peyton Drive last night? I got a friend that lives over there."

"Well," Tyler didn't really want to stand there and launch into the whole thing, but it was too much to hold in. He decided to give her a tidbit.

"It was interesting. The call, as you know, came in at 4:08 AM. We went over there and it was quiet, but all of a sudden we saw movement and we apprehended a suspect with stolen merchandise. He was in possession of a .45-caliber handgun, and we believe he'd burglarized more than one house on the street."

Nick jumped in, stating matter-of-factly, "Now this is where it got weird. We arrived at the tipsters house to ask a few questions."

Nick stopped, looked around and continued, lowering his voice and moving in closer to his rapt audience.

"Apparently a little girl had dreamed the robbery. She even saw the gun and in her dream, the 'perp' was inside the home of her friend. The strange thing is, we don't believe he ever entered that residence. Even stranger, was the fact that the friend was there at our dreamer's house for a sleepover. She was upstairs sleeping while we were there."

He took a breath and looked at her. She was waiting for him to continue, and when he didn't, she said, "That's a bizarre story Nick. Have you two been smoking some of that wacky tobacco you got impounded in the back shed?"

Nick laughed at her. "No. Listen, I have to go run some plates and write a report."

"See ya," Rhonda gave him a small wave.

Tyler lingered a second. He really wanted to talk to her some more, but he needed to get to the chief's office within five minutes.

"Hey Rhonda, I'm thinking about going to see Bad Company at the Family Arena in a few weeks, are you interested in going with me?"

"I'll think about it and get back to you, okay?"

"Okay. Hey, you keep a look out for our witness. The kid is coming in today to give a statement. You'll see her. She looks like a bright-eyed little angel. We saw her this morning and she seems legit. The whole family seems legit as a matter of fact. The grandmother is Rose England, a prominent minister at Rivers Oak Church."

"Thanks, I still think you guys got the report wrong." She laughed and waved him away.

Tyler was pretty confused himself. He didn't really understand exactly what happened last night. He walked off laughing and shaking his head. Rhonda was thinking there was some kind of freaky mystery here. *How could a kid see something in a dream, the cops are dispatched, and they actually catch someone in the act of a burglary?*

It was lunchtime. She was still thoughtful as she went to her locker to get her sandwich and chips. This job was different every day. Some days she didn't have time to take a break, while others went so slow they just seemed to drag. She enjoyed the hectic days, but the quiet ones gave her time to check out anything newsworthy.

As she munched her lunch, she was thinking she would like to see the little girl who had dreams of a robbery that got called in to the police, and actually checked out. It wasn't everyday a person heard a story like that.

It was noon at the compound. Everyone was out on the patio where Carla had set lunch out for them. It was a smorgasbord of crackers, cheese, fruit, and tiny tuna sandwiches.

They were thoughtful during the arrival of June's parents. Skyler had asked her family not to tell anyone unless they had to. It was agreed upon to allow the police to handle alerts in the neighborhood of the burglaries, and the resulting apprehension of the subject.

June and her family had returned home, oblivious of anything out of the ordinary.

Rose was not looking forward to going to the station to give a statement. It was not easy to explain how they knew about this robbery. She just had to tell the truth, as crazy as it sounded.

Skyler finished eating and started running around the yard, playing with the dogs. She was having so much fun giggling and squealing, and everyone laughed as she chased them.

Annie and Jimmy were in a trance as they thought about the things they'd discovered this past year. Their child was gifted somehow, and all they could do was stand by and try to help her cope with it.

Soon the fun ended and it was time to get ready. Rose told Skyler to go wash up to go to the police station. The four of them were going. Rose was so grateful these days that Annie and Jimmy were with her. It was an amazing blessing and she thanked God for it.

It was 1 PM when they entered the lobby and went toward the desk. A woman in civilian clothes with a name badge that read, Rhonda Stiles, asked them if she could help them. Jimmy stepped forward to speak. "We're here to talk to Officer Alan, or Officer Hodges."

Ms. Stiles instructed them to have a seat while she announced their arrival. Within two minutes, a man came around the corner that Rose had met before. He was older and distinguished looking. His hair was cut precisely around his ears and he had an air of authority about him. His name badge read: Robert G. Leigh, Chief of Police. They all stood up as he strolled over to them.

"Hi folks, thanks for coming in. Let's go into my office." They followed him down a series of hallways and into a large office with a dozen pictures on the walls and several trophies in a glass case.

They all took a seat. On his desk was a placard that read, "THE BOSS" which made Rose chuckle a little.

After introductions were made, Chief Leigh addressed Rose. "I remember you, Ms. England. I was so glad when I got the news your granddaughter was home safe." He was smiling kindly at her.

"Your family certainly has gone through a lot. So let's get down to why you're here. I have a report on my desk that I'm a little confused about. The first thing that confuses me is the actual call itself. Can you explain why the report says that Skyler here saw a robbery happening in her dream?"

Rose and Jimmy looked at each other and Jimmy nodded his head for her do the talking.

"Chief, we're aware that it seems far fetched, but the fact is: Skyler has been having visions that awaken her for several years. We've only started to be aware of them since last year. It's some kind of psychic phenomena."

The chief got quiet as he took a moment to jot something down on a piece of paper. An abduction case back in February involving a local woman named, Annie England. He would research that later. He stopped and pursed his mouth in a confused expression.

"Okay. That's a bit hard to swallow, but okay. Have you taken her to a psychiatrist to see what's happening?" he asked.

"Yes, his name is Dr. Matthew Roads."

"I see. This is highly unusual. I don't think I've ever encountered a situation like this. You see we deal with facts here. Witnesses see things with their eyes, not their minds. It is beyond my comprehension." He looked down at his desk and chewed his lip for a minute.

"Can I ask you a few questions, Skyler?" He asked her directly, while looking at Jimmy and Rose for permission.

"Yes." she answered.

"Did you know the man you saw in your dream?"

"No, I don't think so. I didn't see his face. I only know it was a man. In my mind, I saw a tiny bit of a profile and he had a little beard."

"You mean a beard like I have?" The chief was palming his own goatee.

"Yes, kind of."

"So, when you woke up, you told your grandmother?"

"Yes. I went into her room, and told her a man was in June's house. That's my friend June, who was sleeping over with me."

Skyler smiled, thinking about how much fun they had that night.

"Do you think you'd recognize the profile if you saw it again?" He asked her.

"I'm not sure, because it's just a shadow really. Everything's so dark."

"Okay, Honey, thanks for letting me ask you that stuff." The chief turned to Rose, Jimmy and Annie, addressing them now.

"I need a written statement from Skyler. We need everything she can remember. The hand he was using to hold the gun, the size, color and shape of the gun. Every small detail that she can provide us will help to put him behind bars. Even though she was not there, we may have to bring up the fact that she saw him and called the police. Believe me, I wish we could just forget that it happened. It's going to be hard to explain."

They all chuckled a little because that was exactly how they felt.

Chief Leigh looked at Skyler and said, "I believe in miracles. I believe that what is happening with you is some kind of rare gift. I don't understand it, but I do believe it. Just write it all down for me, so I can figure out what to tell the prosecutor when our criminal stands trial in this case."

She nodded her head and spoke to him. Her voice was soft and young. He was staring at her light misty blue eyes thinking he'd never seen such beautiful eyes in all of his days.

"I thank you for believing me. I think I see things to protect my family and friends. It's scary and confusing every time. I don't know why I saw what I saw. I'll write it all down for you the best I can." Then she smiled at him.

He thanked them for coming in.

"Ms. England, if there's anything I can do for you in the future, please call me." He gave Rose his personal card. She nodded and thanked him. He escorted them out to the lobby, where he saluted, turned, and went back in the direction of his office. He had a puzzle to figure out with this case.

Rhonda Stiles stared at the four. They were a very interesting group. The grandmother was dressed very stylishly, and the blonde woman, who she assumed was the girl's mother, was dressed chic as well. The man was striking in a different way. He had tattoos and a hard look about him. The most interesting of them all was the child. Her hair was golden and straight, but when she looked at Rhonda and smiled, there was something ethereal about her glance, as if she could see straight through you.

Later, as Nick passed by, Rhonda stopped him to inquire about the child. "I saw your little dreamer, Nick. What a pretty little thing. You say she made a statement that she saw the robbery while she was sleeping?"

Nick said, "Yup. That's what we got on record. She sees things while she's sleeping. It's pretty far fetched I know. We can't figure it out either. Listen, I have to run, I'll talk to you later okay, Rhonda?" She gave him a thumbs up.

Rhonda was thinking about making a call. First, she needed to spin it to make it a little tastier. There was always a fat envelope full of bills for the juicy morsels she sent over to The Post. She was going to have to wait patiently for more goodies. The child would probably be making a statement. If she could get a look at that, it could be just the treat she needed to get a nice fat envelope.

She put her feet up on a stool under the desk and leaned back for a moment with her arms cradling her head, deep in thought. She uttered to herself, "Momma could really use a new pair of shoes," and smiled. She could just see the headlines, **"Psychic Child Sees Robbery In A Dream And Calls Police"**

Skyler slept soundly after going to the police station. The chief had said he believed her, which made her feel good. Now she was working on her statement. She was hesitating for some reason. Maybe, it was because she knew she could face ridicule at school and even from June. Grandma always told her nothing was better than the truth, so she tried to remember.

> *He was climbing the stairs, and there was brown carpeting. His shoes were sneakers, and they had orange on the back. It was as if I was at the front door watching him. I saw a gun in his right hand, and he had on dark colored gloves, maybe dark gray. He had on a black jacket with some kind of fabric collar, also black. His hair was short and dark colored, a tiny bit curly. He had a hat on, but I could see the hair at the bottom of it. I was watching him from behind and I saw a small beard from the side, but I never saw his face. He was not tall, but more like my dad, on the shorter side. It was like a real dark night in my vision. Then, I woke up and went in to tell my grandma.*

Skyler took the statement down to her dad to read. He was outside getting the grill area cleaned up from the party.

"I finished writing it all down, Dad. It's all I can remember. I never saw his face."

"I'm sure it's fine, Sweetheart. Here, let me take a look." Jimmy slowly read the brief description according to Skyler. It was going to be hard to convince anyone that she saw all of this while she was sleeping. Jimmy talked to her calmly, while digging around in a drawer full of mailing materials. He put her statement into an envelope.

"Don't worry about anything. Everything will be fine. If you want, we can take it to the chief later."

"I sure hope no one at school finds out about my visions, Dad. I don't think I could take it if they all stared at me like I was some kind of a freak."

"They won't, Sky. No need to get all worried about it. Hey, do you want to go with Bo and I in a little while? He's going to take me out driving." Jimmy scrunched up his face as if he were scared.

Those expressions made Sky giggle, and took her mind off the events of the other night.

"Yea sure, I have to see this. I'll be back in a minute Dad; I'm going to take Matilda down to the lake, she needs a walk."

Annie was watching the two of them from inside the kitchen. She was amazed at how much her life had changed since she was abducted almost six months ago. It seemed like years had passed since she danced in Illinois. One thing was for sure: she was staying right here. Her family needed her and it was like glue to her. Nothing could pry her away from any of them now.

She watched Skyler running up the yard toward her father, laughing and yelling, "Dad, watch!" as she ran in circles with the little dog on her heels. It was as if Annie were seeing her daughter for the first time.

Annie's eyes welled up with tears. How many times had Skyler woke up frightened and she wasn't here? So many years of mothering the kids wasted. She couldn't help beating herself up. She should be the one her baby girl cries out for, but she isn't. Her baby cries out for Rose. Annie took out a tissue to blow her nose, still pondering on her life. She vowed things would change drastically. She was very anxious to be a good mother now.

Bo came home from working at the supermarket in town. He was seventeen now, and he was chomping at the bit to get his driver's license. He yelled for his father, "Dad, I'm home. Where are you?"

He heard, "Out here, Son, on the patio."

Bo came out, and saw Skyler running around with the dogs on her heels, laughing. It was a sound that made him smile as he addressed his father. "Dad, are we still going to go out driving? I want to take my test this Saturday, okay?"

Jimmy looked at his son. He was taller than Jimmy by two inches already. He smiled and answered him.

"Yes, and Sky wants to go with us. We're going to the police station to drop off her statement to the chief, then we'll let you drive around a while."

"Cool, I'm going to change. How long till you guys are ready?"

"Well, you just let me know when you're ready, and we'll go."

Jimmy watched as Bo bounded up the stairs to change. He remembered back to when he got his license, how excited he was. He went in to find Rose. He needed to talk to her about which car she wanted Bo to be driving when he took his test.

Rose was in her office, writing a sermon for this Sunday's worship service. Jimmy tapped on the door and heard, "Come in."

He went in slowly, smiling at her. "Hi Rose, got a minute?"

"Of course, what's up Jimmy?" She swiveled the leather chair toward him, giving him her full attention.

"I'm taking Sky and Bo to the police station to drop off Skyler's statement, then I'm turning the wheel over to Bo. He needs to practice driving. I was wondering if we should take the Rover, so he could take his test in it Saturday. I'm going to let him try parallel parking today."

"That sounds like a great idea. How's he doing with the practice so far?" She'd taken him driving a few times, but now it was getting serious. The boy needed to have a lot more time behind the wheel.

"Well, I think he's about ready, but I don't want him to try and park the Escalade. I thought the Rover would be best."

"That's fine. Are you taking him Saturday to take the test?" she asked.

"That's the goal. You're welcome to come with us."

"Oh well thanks, but you guys can handle that. Did I ever tell you how much it means to me that you're here? It means a lot Jimmy, I'm grateful. You guys be careful okay?"

"You bet Rose. Will we see you at dinner?" he asked, as he backed out of the room.

"Oh yes, Carla's making my favorite: salmon patties with fresh zucchini. See you all later."

Jimmy nodded his head at her and bounded down the stairs to get the Rover keys and bring the car around to the front of the house. What an amazing life he had here with Rose, Annie, and the kids. He never wanted to leave.

Annie came out of her room, just as Bo was coming out of his.

"Hi Mom, how are you today?" He stopped and looked at her.

"I'm fine Bo, just been tired a lot and worried about your sister. How about you? Are you doing okay today?" she asked. They turned to walk down the stairs together, chatting all the way down.

"I'm great, Dad's taking me driving in a few minutes. I'm so ready to get my license, then Carla won't have to run me to work and back."

"She doesn't mind, Bo." Annie told him.

Just then Cleo pounced at Annie, wanting to play. She reached down to pick up the cat, crooning to it. "What are you up to Cleo? Silly boy. You want some kitty treats?"

Annie and Bo were heading toward the kitchen, where Jimmy was waiting for the kids. After giving Cleo a treat and patting him on the head, Annie turned to Jimmy.

"So, you're taking Bo driving today?" she asked.

Jimmy smiled at her. He still thought she was the most beautiful woman he'd ever seen. His heart fluttered sometimes when he looked at her.

"I'm going to make sure he's ready for his test on Saturday. We are taking the Rover today. I think he can ace parallel parking with that."

Annie felt really happy for her son. She was overwhelmed with maternal instincts these days. As she stood there with Jimmy and Bo, it hit her that she wanted to be with them. Not just today, but always. She never wanted to be away from any of them again.

It was a moment that sobered her. This was her son getting ready to drive off into the sunset. She wanted to make sure he would always be safe.

"I'll tell you what Bo, you can be my personal chauffeur once you get your license, okay? I'll even pay you."

Bo laughed. "Okay, you've got a deal. First I'm going to have to save up for a car."

Annie said, "You know Bo, I'm not really using my Fusion very much. You can drive it any time, as long as I don't need it, okay? I might be getting a job in the near future, but until then, I'll share it." She smiled at him and reached up to touch his shoulder.

Bo smiled real big, "Really? Thanks, Mom; it's a pretty cool car. That's awesome." Jimmy was watching the two, smiling from ear to ear.

Skyler came in then with the envelope in her hand. "I'm ready to go Dad, should I tell Grandma we're leaving?"

"No, I was talking to her a little while ago." Jimmy said. "She's all good with us going. We'll all be together at dinner later. Come on, girl."

He picked up the keys and headed toward the door. Annie stopped him. "Wait, Jimmy," She took a few steps over and kissed him on the cheek and whispered, "You're pretty special you know."

Jimmy paused a moment, relishing the feeling of her affection. He felt a strong impulse to grab her and hug her, but that would have ruined it. He couldn't stop smiling, "Thank you, ma'am, you're not so bad yourself."

The two kids were watching this exchange. They were frozen, absorbing something they had not seen here before. Their mom and dad were making googly eyes at each other. They looked back and forth, then shrugged and smiled. It was all good.

Jimmy waited in the car, while Skyler and Bo took the statement into the station. They left it with the woman at the desk. It was in a manila envelope that was sealed with a thin piece of nylon-threaded tape. It said, "Chief Robert Leigh, Private" on the front. Then they bounded back out where their dad was waiting for them, and headed out for Bo's driving lesson.

Rhonda Stiles picked up the large envelope and turned it over to study the seal. She was thinking about doing something she shouldn't. She was going to read the statement and reseal it. No one would ever know, and the chief probably wouldn't mind that much. She really wanted to see what the little girl said.

She slipped it under her sweater and up under her arm, holding it secure. She headed for the ladies room. Once behind the locked door, she pulled out a nail file she'd put into her pocket, and began gently picking at the corner of the packing tape. The seal gave easily and she gently tugged at it, being extremely careful not to rip or tear the envelope.

Her eyes scanned the brief statement and she twisted her mouth up in confusion.

Maybe she missed something, but how could a witness see all of this when they were seven miles away, sleeping?

Rhonda was in disbelief. She sat there a moment figuring out what she should do. She'd better get this back up front and into the chief's mail slot, she didn't want to get caught opening it.

There was a dilemma if she leaked this information. The family and the chief would try and find out who was responsible. He had questioned her before when the press got a hold of details that had not been released to the public, and she'd acted completely surprised. She needed to sit on it for now, and not act too precipitously. The money was not worth her job. She was curious, that was for sure.

After putting the manila envelope where it was supposed to be, she sat down at her desk and resumed her day. The statement was gnawing at her, though. Allegedly, Skyler Conrad had envisioned a robbery that never happened; coincidentally a perpetrator was arrested two doors down that fit the description she gave. Skyler claimed she saw all of this while she was asleep seven miles away.

Back at the compound, Rose got a phone call from Dr. Roads. He had a friend he wanted to introduce them to. She was a medium, and authored a book entitled, Seeing and Believing. Her name was Emily Stone. Matthew made a request of Rose, asking her to allow Emily to meet the family at Sky's next session.

That evening, Rose told everyone about the request. "What do you think, Grandma?" asked Sky.

"I'm not sure about mediums, but I'm going to keep an open mind. There's something supernatural going on here, and I guess to find answers, we have to turn to the experts in the field."

Rose looked around the room at the four faces.

"What are you all thinking about a medium observing the next session?" She asked.

"I'll check her out, Mom." Annie told her. "Maybe I can purchase her book on Amazon and have it shipped here. What day is the appointment set for?"

"Next Monday, at 2:30 PM, after Sky gets out of school." Rose smiled at Annie. She was also watching Sky, who was listening to all of this, while quietly feeding Martin and Matilda scraps of fish under the table.

"Let's do some research and talk at dinner in a few days. I'm going to order her book."

Jimmy said, "I have mixed feelings, because it's hard to know if we can trust her. Then, there's the fact that I'm a huge skeptic, but that certainly has changed." Jimmy laughed at himself.

Rose assured them, "I trust Matthew to keep his word and keep this from going public. I'm curious about the woman. It could be quite interesting to hear what she says. One thing I'm completely sure of is the fact that God is in control here. He has a purpose for everything. I'm going to have faith, while continuing to allow the field experts to explain things to me."

Bo was thoughtful. A lot had been said. He was feeling protective again. He didn't want strangers watching his sister during her sessions, but if his grandmother approved, he would trust her instincts.

"Mom," he said, "If you get the book, I'd like to read it, okay?"

"Oh, okay, we can all read it and get a feel for what kind of a woman this Emily Stone is. I'm going to be there as well, Mom." Annie told Rose.

So it was decided. Rose called Dr. Roads to tell him the family was on board with the medium being present at the next session.

12

Meeting Emily

She wasn't just any medium. Emily was renowned in Canada where she grew up. Her face was in the paper and on the news. Over fifteen missing person cases were solved as a result of Emily's assistance. She had earned the respect of her countrymen by the time she was twenty-two years old.

Emily Stone came to the U.S. to attend journalism school. She attended the university in Columbia, Missouri, where she met Matthew Roads. He studied her, testing and documenting results. She was astounding to him. A proven clairvoyant, she was a rare example, and one of the first substantiated cases of supernatural abilities he himself had ever encountered.

After receiving her degree, she wrote a book, which was published and immediately took its place on the New York Times' best-sellers list.

Matthew asked her to be present. He knew Emily was an invaluable expert on the subject of paranormal psychosis. He wanted her evaluation on Skyler's inordinate case.

As a very young child, Emily realized she had the gift of sight.

One of the first incidences was when her family was at the zoo. She was holding her mother's hand one minute, and suddenly let go to begin running. As her mom took off after her, they stumbled through a narrow pathway that led to a wooded area. The scene was startling; a man was hurting a woman. The woman was on the ground and he was on top of her, hitting her repeatedly.

Mrs. Stone started screaming and people started running over to the violent scene happening in the overgrown area. Emily was quickly pulled away, while the man, seeing a crowd forming, fled, leaving his victim lying there in shock.

It had almost resulted in rape, and would have, if the little girl hadn't exposed it. Five minutes earlier, the woman had come out of the Ladies room. The unidentified man struck her over the head, and pulled her into the brush. He held his hand over her mouth, and continued to hit her over the head and in the face. No one had realized she was gone.

Park rangers and police questioned the child. She maintained that she felt the woman crying. When they asked her if she saw where he had taken the woman, she said, "No. I just knew where the woman was, because I felt her. In my mind, I felt her crying and I heard where it was coming from,"

Emily was six years old. The next year, there was another dramatic event. Just as unexplainable.

A little boy had wandered off in a town nearby. People searched all night and it was feared that he might have been abducted. Emily came into the kitchen on the second day of the search, and made a statement that shocked her father.

"Eli's in a hole, Daddy." Her father asked, "How do you know Emily?"

"I can hear him in my mind. I feel him crying and he's in a deep dark hole."

Mr. Stone called the authorities. When they arrived, they asked Emily if she saw or felt anything else about Eli.

She looked right at them, and said, "His daddy dug the hole."

They were stunned. As they continued to explore the lead, it was discovered that Eli's father had dug a well for the neighbor a half-mile away. The house was not finished, and no one had searched that property.

They found the child in the hole. He had wandered down there looking for his father. He was only five.

The newspapers wanted to interview the Stone family. The town expressed gratitude and curiosity toward Emily. The questions continued, but there was never an answer they could easily accept. Emily had unexplainable abilities. She was special.

Several years went by. She was helping the police find 'missing' children, in which she gave viable descriptions of the abductor in multiple cases. Her efforts were lauded and she was a town hero.

It was a curse for her sometimes. There were cases she couldn't solve. She felt like a failure, and wanted to run and hide from the people seeking answers she couldn't always give.

She felt people, and knew what they were going to say to her before they said it. Her friends at school wanted her to 'read' them all of the time.

Her good friend John came to her one day with a request. He wanted her to help him locate his father. He'd been searching for several years. His mother told him everything she knew. She'd met Tom in Florida, while he was working on a shrimp boat. Their two-year affair ended badly and she lost contact with him. The last known address was in Charleston, South Carolina.

John had a hat from his dad. It was a gift he'd received when he was six. Now, at seventeen, it was the only thing connecting him to his father.

They sat in the park at a picnic table. Emily held the hat and closed her eyes. She smelled the salty sea right away, and knew he'd stayed near the ocean. There were other pictures flashing through her mind. She saw a young man in a sailor suit, then it changed and she saw his face as it is now. It was weathered from the elements and she was seeing from his eyes as he gazed out into the ocean waves, watching and listening to the gulls.

Emily opened her eyes and smiled at John. "He's alive, living somewhere in the Gulf of Mexico for sure. I saw a sign that said Orange Beach. Also, your father was in the Navy. You'll find him in Alabama somewhere. There's a strong smell of fish, and sea gulls everywhere, so he lives near or even on a beach."

John was excited to start the search and a week later she got a call from him. He'd located his father, who was living in Gulf Shores,

Alabama, where he had his own seafood shipping business. He'd served ten years in the United States Navy. John was traveling down to meet him next month.

Every day was a new day for Emily Stone. She'd written and published her book, "Seeing And Believing." Now, she was on a search to find others like her. There was barely a handful that had an authentic gift. From what she heard Dr. Roads say, his patient Skyler Conrad had some highly unique abilities. She was going to meet her on Monday.

Rose, Annie, Jimmy and Skyler were sitting in the lounge awaiting Matthew and his friend. As they arrived, Skyler smiled at Matthew. She loved him.

"Hi Skyler. What's kickin', chicken?" He said to her, smiling.

She replied, "No Matthew, its, 'what's shakin' bacon?" and started giggling.

Emily thought she was utterly charming. Her giggle was sweet and it made Emily want to tickle her to hear it again.

Matthew began introducing everyone. Emily nodded and shook hands with the family, ever aware of the gaze of Skyler.

As they all sat down in the spacious office, Matthew said, "I'm curious if any of you have read Emily's book. I know we talked about it."

"Yes." Annie replied, "We've all read your book, Ms. Stone. It's truly amazing!"

"Oh wow, thank you. I wasn't expecting that. Please, call me Emily."

"Okay, and you can call me Annie. I found it fascinating. It makes me think that maybe our baby isn't alone. There's someone else that understands this phenomena."

"Yes, I hear you. You're right. I'm already picking up some very subtle messages about you and your family. Don't be put out by that, it's normal for me. As I get more familiar with you, the messages get more accurate and more personal."

"Do you see things while you're awake?" asked Sky.

"Yes, I sure do. Right now, I'm seeing something about you."

"What?" asked Sky, completely intrigued.

"I see you sitting on a swing. You have a small dog that you're talking to."

"Oh my gosh, that's amazing. What else?"

Emily started laughing. "I'm here to observe you with Dr. Roads today, but, if you want me to read you, I will. I need permission to do that from your parents though, okay?"

Skyler said, "Okay." She really liked Emily already. It was going to be really fun to talk to her about the crazy stuff she saw.

Rose was eager to talk to Emily as well, but she waited patiently as Matthew started his session with Sky.

He began, "Today, I want to talk about the very first time you remember having a vision. Do you remember it?"

"I never knew I was having visions. My brother Bo was riding the four-wheeler one time while I was taking a nap and I woke up convinced he'd wrecked. I went downstairs to ask Carla where he was and she said, "Outside playing." I was watching television an hour later when he came in bleeding. He had rolled the ATV when he hit a log, and landed in some stickers. I never knew it was a vision, I just thought it was normal."

"What else do you remember?"

"The time Bo was getting ready to go skating with Billy. I was asleep on the couch and I woke up because I saw a man watching Bo. He was just a shadow, but he was bad. I told Carla, and she told Bo to call her when it was over, she would come in and get them. That night a boy named Richard was snatched while he was outside waiting for his ride. The bad man was caught within hours and Richard was with him in the car. He was watching Bo and Billy though."

"How does it feel when these premonitions wake you, Skyler?"

"It's like I'm seeing a movie. Usually there's a bright light and then just shadows in motion. When the coyote was in the yard, I felt it and knew what it wanted. It was coming after Matilda. That was scary. I never knew until the next day that it was real. I was six. The next scariest was when I saw Grandma's plane crash. I was seven."

"How did you feel then, Sky?"

"Petrified and desperate to make sure I could talk to her. I called her right away. It was in the middle of the night and she wouldn't listen. Then I called her again at 5 AM. I was so upset and she still kept telling me it was going to be okay, but I knew it wasn't. I knew what was going to happen to that plane."

On the sofa, Rose was shaking her head. Jimmy put his arm around her, comforting her as they listened attentively.

"You're doing much better now that you can talk about the visions, aren't you?" Matthew was sitting directly across from her. It felt like they were alone in the room as he directed his forthright gaze at her, engaging her.

"I'm afraid to fall asleep sometimes. I have fear about stuff. When I was kidnapped and taken away from my grandma, it was the scariest thing that has ever happened. I saw it all in a vision, but I just didn't know when it was going to happen. That's the worst thing. Seeing something bad, but not knowing when it will happen."

Matthew told her he asked Emily her so that Skyler would understand she was not alone. Although rare, others were experiencing unexplainable premonitions. He asked everyone in the room if they would like Emily to read Sky.

Rose said she was okay with it, as well as Jimmy and Annie.

"What about you, Skyler? How do you feel about this?"

"I want to hear what she says." She smiled over at Emily, who was sitting quietly during the exchange. "I want to know why I'm seeing things that no one else sees. Nobody seems to understand why."

Matthew asked Emily to take his chair, directly in front of his patient. He went over to the side couch, next to Rose.

The room was silent a moment as Emily got situated in her new location, and took Sky's hands in hers. She instructed her softly to clear her mind and just think about her dog. It was an eerie feeling for Rose, Jimmy, and Annie as they observed. The only sounds were those echoing from beyond the room, as Emily stared into the brilliant eyes of the child before her.

She began blinking and nodding. Her eyes filled with tears and her expressions flooded her face like a kaleidoscope. She was obviously receiving some kind of images.

The audience waited, enthralled with the scene before them. Matthew was jotting notes continuously, while Rose silently called on God to sanction the decision to allow this stranger to do a spiritual reading. She heard, "hmm" and a few other barely audible sounds, as Emily saw things no one else saw.

Approximately four minutes passed, and Jimmy was thinking it was longer than all of his eight years in prison. He was about to jump out of his seat with apprehension.

Emily finally let go of Sky's hands and sat back a moment, seeming to gather her thoughts. She reached behind her and took a drink of water from the glass that was on the desk.

She started to talk then, her voice shaky and low. The occupants in the room all seemed to unconsciously move closer, if even an inch, to hear her clearly

"This is phenomenal. I will try to convey to you all what I've seen." She nodded at Matthew, who stood with pen and pad, writing everything down. The session was also being recorded.

The three adults that loved this child the most were on the edge of their seats, waiting to hear what this unusually gifted woman was about to say. They were feeling unease at this point. The fear of the unknown was choking them; yet the revelation was even more frightening.

Emily looked at everyone and knew what she was about to reveal would rock them to their cores.

"I must warn you, what I'm about to say is going to sound like something out of the twilight zone. It will shock you all, and it'll be hard to digest." She took a moment, trying to find the words to go on.

"There was a woman that lived two generations back, named Marie. Rose, who was she?"

"She was my grandmother. Her name was Marie Anne Baxter. Skyler's middle name is Marie, after her."

Emily nodded smiling. She took a deep breath, choosing her words carefully.

"When Skyler was born, Marie's soul inhabited her spirit. She lives and dwells with Skyler. Listen carefully to what I'm about to tell you: Marie has inhabited Skyler's spirit, to be a guardian to you all."

You could have heard a pin drop as the family took on glazed looks. They were trying to understand the statement.

"Oh Lord, have mercy on our souls." Rose reverted to prayer, asking God to help her understand His will here. She closed her eyes a moment, shaking her head. Emily gave them all a second to absorb the information before continuing the explanation.

"Every vision has a purpose. It's to protect and do only good, and ward off evil. Marie is watching over you, Rose. She's here now. She's present in spirit. She's been reincarnated through Skyler."

Even Matthew was aghast. He was shaking his head and felt emotion well up. A tear slid down his face. In the past ten years of psychoanalysis, he'd never encountered anything of this caliber. It flooded him with joy to hear what Emily was saying.

A box of tissue was quietly passed around the room. There were sniffles, and as the family realized what she was saying, they started to look around at one another.

"I realize it's a lot to take in. I feel that we're witnessing a miracle. The revelation is there in Skyler's eyes. I've been given a special gift to be able to see it. The fact is: Marie is gazing at all of us right now."

Skyler, who'd been quiet, now started speaking to everyone. Her childish voice had no fear. In fact, it held wonder.

"I guess that makes sense. My great great grandma is showingme things, so I can keep our family safe. I'm kind of happy that she's with me. Grandma, can we see pictures of her when we get home?"

"Yes, we can." Rose held her arms open and Skyler went over and sat on her lap. As she was being held, she reached her hand over to her mother as well, who was sitting next to Rose.

Emily stood, telling them she was just a phone call away if they needed her. She thanked them for allowing her to meet Sky, and reveal what she saw. They hugged and shook hands.

Matthew told them he was just as chilled by the session today as they were. He still wanted to see Skyler next Monday.

The day had given them an answer they sought. Every person in the room had just been introduced to an entity they could not see.

13
Security Breach

Rose was in her office working on the following Sunday's sermon. She was feeling isolated. There were very few that she could share the information she'd just been given with.

Her sermon was going to be about faith this week. One of her very favorite quotes read:

"Faith is taking the next step, even if you cannot see the stairway"

She'd lived her life according to this quote. She was going to continue believing and having faith in the things she could not see.

It was difficult explaining what Emily Stone picked up, to Bo and Carla; the reading stunned them. Carla did not want to believe a spirit was living in Skyler. Rose laughed at her as she started to make the sign of the cross and back away.

Rose reassured her, and Skyler said, "It's alright, Carla. She's a good spirit. She's my grandmother; it's kind of a miracle. You shouldn't be so scared of things."

Bo was conditioned by now to hearing unusual claims. He was flooded with several emotions. One of them was relief that therewas an explanation, as bizarre as it was. The other emotion was protectiveness. He didn't know how to keep Sky safe. Since her kidnapping, he slept lighter. It was still his job as her big brother to look after her, and he always would.

Skyler sat on the sofa between Annie and Rose as they looked at old photos of Marie Anne Baxter. She was a gorgeous woman, tall and slender.

"You're built just like her Annie. She was always very elegant in stature, you inherited her graceful carriage." Rose tried to remember some of the things she knew about her grandmother.

"She was a suffragette. That's a woman who protested and marched, fighting for women's rights. Back in her day, a woman could not smoke, drink, or vote. As the women revolted, they won the right to vote and eventually the other things came along.

She was married for thirty-five years to my grandfather, Roy Baxter. They had two children, Miriam, who was my mother and your uncle Philip."

"Let's see, what else. Grandma Marie very active with starting the P.T.A. in her community. She went door-to-door, gathering parents of students at the local school. She formed the committee and strengthened the curriculum. We know these things because she left a journal that my mother read when she passed away. She was a very strong woman, always advocating for kids and people who couldn't speak for themselves."

"Wow Mom, that's amazing." Annie was pretty impressed with her great grandmother. "I see where you get your gumption from."

They all laughed at that. Skyler was thinking she didn't really know what gumption was, but she was sure her grandma had it.

As Skyler looked at the photos, she felt funny. This woman was giving her something that allowed her to see bad things that were going to happen. It made sense in a way. She wanted to protect them all. Skyler didn't mind it so much, except that it made her different. She was not the same as her friends or her family.

Rose's gumption was about to be tested a few mornings later. She walked down to get her newspaper and brought it to her favorite place in the breakfast room to read. As she looked at the headlines of the day, her eyes fell on a story. The title read, "**Local Girl Sees Robbery While Sleeping.**"

The story didn't mention any names, but Rose felt betrayed. How did the press get a hold of this? She went into her office and called the Police Department. When the receptionist answered, Rose asked to speak with the chief. As she sat on hold listening to elevator music, it occurred to her that she needed to take a moment and think it through. She hung up.

She sat there praying silently for an answer. She would consult the others at dinner tonight. There was a fine line to keeping the family's secret. Rose needed to prepare herself. She would have to explain a lot to her church family, if Skyler's unusual gift was revealed. She'd continue to fight for the privacy of her home.

It occurred to her to call Emily, so that's what she did. Emily listened to Rose's dilemma and her heart went out to her. The issue of privacy had been blown out of the water when Emily's gift was discovered.

"I understand, Rose. Believe me I do. My parents were thrust into the public spotlight after I solved the case of the missing boy, Eli Phinney. It was a barrage of media, and nothing could have prepared me for what was happening. I was a freak in my town. At first I hid and withdrew, but after a while I realized I could help others. That's when I embraced it."

Rose felt better, and thanked her. It was a hard thing to hear, but Rose knew that if they were forced, they would all make the decision together to go public. It would be difficult and they would have to be strong.

At dinner that evening, Rose told her family about the story in the local paper.

"It's highly probable that our identity could be leaked. I need everyone to be aware of this. We need to talk about the media and how we can all be prepared if we are forced to make a statement."

"I feel scared, Grandma. What if everyone knows about me?"

"I want you to remember how Emily handled it, Skyler. She had the news people and the whole town counting on her to use her gift to help find missing people. Imagine how that was for her. If all of this gets out, then we'll call Dr. Roads and he can help us explain it, okay?"

"Okay." She smiled and took her dishes to the kitchen. On the way, she heard the dogs barking at something outside the door.

Skyler slid open the door, peering into the twilight. There was someone out there. Someone was on the fence, with binoculars, looking toward the house. Skyler slammed the door shut and went into the dining area.

"Someone's out there Grandma! Look over there, by the fence. I saw them."

Rose jumped out of her chair and went to the door. Jimmy, Bo, and Annie followed on her heels. She got her flashlight and shone it around the back of the compound. She saw a movement and went to the phone, dialing the police.

"I want to report a trespasser, hurry." She gave them the address.

They all filed into the family room, huddling close while watching the great wall of windows that looked out over the grounds. Rose called Ben, her head of security and told him there was an intruder by the fence line near the copse of river birch. They left the lights off, quieting the dogs. Soon they heard a buzzer and Rose opened the gate. The police had arrived, Ben was right behind them.

A search was on, and although the trespasser was long gone, they found footprints all along the back of the property. The parameter had been breached by a stranger and Rose was livid.

"How come we didn't get an alarm, Ben?" she demanded.

"The alarm was overridden somehow, electronically. I'm thinking the intruder has knowledge of the software we're using and has hacked our program. We'll install extra firewalls Rose, don't worry."

"You'd better, Ben. I have some very valuable things here, the most of which are my family!"

"Yes ma'am, I'll address it right away."

"We've taken some photos of the footprints, Ms. England." The police were trying to ease her nerves. "We'll also view your surveillance footage to see if we can get an ID on the subject."

"We believe the trespasser came in on foot. There's only one set of prints, so he or she was alone. We'll continue to patrol the entire area throughout the night. Call us if there are any more episodes, okay?"

"Thank you, I'm sorry to be so agitated, I'm just so rattled. This should not be happening. Bo and Jimmy, who'd been standing by came closer to console Rose.

"It's going to be okay, Rose. Don't worry." Jimmy was trying to calm her down.

"I can't take it if someone gets inside the compound Jimmy, it's not okay."

"I know. Listen, let's go get some cocoa and go into the media room. The police and Ben are taking care of this. Come on."

Rose let him lead her into the back of the house, everyone trailing behind her, worried for her.

Skyler stood back, wondering if it was because of her that someone was trying to watch them, or photograph them. She grabbed Matilda up and held her tightly, then proceeded in to gather with the others.

Across town, Rhonda Stiles opened the door of her apartment at the knock.

"Well, how did it go? Did you get any pictures of the little girl?" She stood questioning the young man dressed in black. He took off his stocking cap and sat down, winded.

"No. That place is remote. I had to walk through some dense crap to stay hidden, and then, there are two yappy dogs in the house.

I heard them right before I saw the sliding glass door open and a child peering out trying to see me. I had to hightail it out of that place and it's good thing I did; as I was coming down around the final curve, I saw the police. That was a close call. I could have gotten caught, Rhonda, and arrested for trespassing."

"Shit! There goes my paycheck. This was supposed to be easy money. So did you get any pictures at all? I told you there's a story here. This little girl has some kind of psychic power or something."

"Calm down, I got you a few pictures of the house. The light was bad though, I don't think you can use them for anything."

"Okay, but, I'm telling you, Lonnie, someone's going to get wind of this and it's going to command a high price if we can get a picture of that little girl!"

"She has to leave that fortress sometime. Have some patience, I'll get the shots."

"Okay, but if you flub this up, I'll get someone else. I want a photo to go along with the back-up story I leaked to the press."

Lonnie had wasted an entire night, trying to get the goods for Rhonda. He was tired and needed a drink.

"Listen, I'll give you a call if I get anything worth using. I got to hit it, talk at you later."

"Okay, well, just lay low for a while. I'll call you next week." Rhonda let him out and closed the door. She snapped the dead bolt in place thinking, "*you never know what kind of nut jobs are lurking around,*" then she laughed at the irony of her own thoughts.

Rose was exhausted. There had been several times she felt insecure, but ever since Skyler was taken, things had become more serious. She would beef up security; maybe even hire someone to patrol the grounds hourly. Whatever it took, she was not going to give anyone an opportunity to attack her home or her family.

The police didn't have much to go on. The intruder would most likely never be found. Rose felt like turning every light off and sitting in the dark, watching through the great windows. No one in the house would sleep very soundly for a while.

Chief Leigh had seen the paper this morning as well. He knew that someone had leaked it to the press. There were only a handful of people at the station who knew about the call and the little girls story: his two best patrolmen, and the staff in charge of filing all calls and statements into record.

The call that an intruder had breached the property was disturbing him. He was concerned for the child. He remembered her face and eyes. She was real special. Just thinking about her sweet little smile and voice made him feel calm, like taking a child for a walk and bonding in the most essential way. If she were his child, he would want to protect her from the scum that would make her a target and exploit her. He felt sad, but certain that eventually, Skyler Conrad's gift would be exposed.

School was back in and it was picture day today. Jimmy was driving the kids in this morning. He looked at them when they came into the kitchen and whistled.

"Wow, you two look so nice. I swear you look more like your mom everyday, Skyler. Bo, you do look a little like your old man, only better looking. I'm one proud Daddy."

They grabbed their books and bags and piled into the car.

"Sky, I don't want you waiting outside by the fence with your friends today. I need you to be at the front steps, okay?"

"How come, Dad?" she asked in her sweet innocent voice.

"Just stay near the building for a while. We need to keep you safe. Every since the kidnapping we've been scared to let you out of our sight. I'm sure everything's fine, but just for a while; can you stay up on the steps till we come? Please?"

"Sure, Dad, but don't worry, it's safe here at school." She smiled at him and as they pulled up to the drop off point, she said, "I love you, Daddy." She kissed him quickly on the cheek before scrambling out, and Jimmy felt like an ice-cream cone on a hot summer day. He was melting straight into the seat.

"I love you guys. See you later, have a great day."

He watched them. Bo escorted his sister up the steps, then bounded down and flew toward his school on the other side of the parking lot.

Jimmy couldn't be any happier these days. He'd missed way too much of their lives. From now on, he was going to be right there, all the time. He headed off to Main Street. He had a job interview at Dobbs this morning. Rose knew the owners and she told him he would get the job as long as he went over today and applied himself.

Today was a good day for Annie as well. She was helping Rose start a garden. The little dogs were lying in the sunshine, lazily watching them. Rose was on her knees, wearing a huge hat and gloves. She talked to Annie as she dug in the dirt, depositing seeds.

"I had six tomato plants last year, Annie, and zucchini. Carla and I made a salad almost every night until the kids were sick of them. Bo sure loves tomatoes. He slices them and puts them on bread with just a little salad dressing and pepper. I told him he was going to turn into a tomato." She was chuckling as she thought about the boy's appetite.

"What about Skyler, Mom? Does she like salad much?"

"Oh yea, your kids are not picky when it comes to eating. Carla is a very good cook. She knows how to flavor food. I got lucky the day she walked up to the door with a resume in her hand."

"Doesn't Carla have any family, Mom?"

"Yes, her daughter, Angelina, she's 29. She lives in Illinois and she's a nurse. When Carla came to me, she was divorced and her daughter was off at school. We needed each other."

Rose sat up on her knees a minute, rubbing her back.

"She was living in a small apartment in town by herself. I had put a want ad in the local gazette asking for an experienced housekeeper/nanny and she came to the house. My Lord, that was eight years ago. Where has all the time gone to?"

"I'm thirsty, Mom. How about a nice Pepsi or 7-up to wet your whistle?"

"That sounds lovely. I'll be right here."

Rose's phone was ringing. She took off her dirty garden gloves to answer it. It was Chief Leigh.

"Hello Chief, what's up?"

"I just wanted to see how you all have been doing. I saw the paper, Ms. England. I'm sorry that someone has decided to print a story about the events of the other night. I'm also aware that you all had an intruder at your place, and he or she has not been caught."

"I'm just hanging by my fingernails over this Chief, worried about the public becoming aware of Skyler's gift. I swear it's causing me to lose sleep, and not much does that." She laughed a little.

"Well, I just wanted to call and ask if I could come out and see the compound. I'm feeling protective toward your little gal."

"Oh sure, Chief. When would you like to come by?"

"Please call me Robert, Ma'am, if you don't mind."

"Okay, Robert, and please, call me Rose."

"Sure, Ms. England, I mean, Rose." He was laughing. It was a sound she liked.

"Listen, we have dinner at 6 PM, would you like to join us tonight, Robert?"

"Tonight? Why yes, sure would. I know where you are. See you then, Ma'am, I mean, Rose."

Rose could hear the smile on his face. There was some kind of attractive male vibrato in his voice as well. It made her feel warm and comforted. She liked Chief Leigh very much.

"Who was that, Mom? Anybody important?"

"It was the Chief of Police. He's paying us a social call this evening. I invited him to dinner."

Annie just stared at her. "Oh," was all she said. Any answers she sought were there on her mother's face. Rose was blushing and it was a good look on her.

Back at the small apartment in town, Rhonda Stiles was chewing her fingernails. She'd found out about Skyler's kidnapping back in March. As she viewed the details of the report, she read the child's statement. Skyler said: Mr. Samuels let her go the next morning. He was a nice man with two little girls, she was not afraid of him.

Rhonda had seen her. The child was definitely unusual. There was another report here that had to do with her mother, Annie England. She'd been rescued after an attempted abduction in February. The report listed a timeline of her rescue. There was a call into the station 5 minutes after she was taken, and she was rescued 15 minutes later. Annie England was found after a claim from Skyler that her mom was going to be thrown into the Mississippi River.

This was a mystery, and Rhonda needed to figure it out. She felt there was something supernatural with the child, something nobody knew.

14
Meeting Robert

Rose was taking the Chief on a tour around the grounds. The sheer beauty of it astounded him. The hill beyond the house dipped gracefully into a valley and beyond. The lake shimmered with the golden rays of the sun bouncing on it, in motion with the small boats and crafts bobbing in the breeze. Rose was proud of her home.

Chief Robert Leigh was quite taken with this handsome woman. He was a widower; however, he felt like he was married to his job.

As he strolled with her, he was comfortable and relaxed. She seemed to be a remarkable lady.

"Were you ever married? I mean, if you don't mind me asking." He started casually conversing with her.

"No, on both counts." Rose hadn't been asked that in many years. She was not used to a man paying her attention. It felt nice; she didn't mind it at all.

"I guess the years were just filled up with my vocation. Once I answered the call to the pulpit, the time was always full. I've been raising the children for the last nine years as well. It's been a wonderful life. I've traveled a lot, but recently I decided to decrease my out of town engagements. The family has been through some harrowing things this past year."

They'd reached the gazebo and she was glad she'd placed a blanket on the bench. The evening had gained a chill. They sat with a comfortable distance between them and continued their visit.

"I'm completely taken with your little Skyler, Rose. I never had any children of my own. Ava's son who's oh…thirty-four I think, is married, and they live in Colorado. When Ava passed away, my relationship with them seemed to evaporate. They don't have any kids yet."

"How did Ava die, Robert? If you don't mind my asking."

He smiled, as he answered her gentle question.

"No, it's okay. She had lung cancer. She was a smoker; two packs a day, we both were. We would sit outside on nights like this and enjoy our smoke. The day she got diagnosed we both quit, but it was too late. I lost her, but we had thirty-one good years together. She always thought she would be the widow, with me being a cop. Hmm." He was actually enjoying the sharing with Rose.

"How very sad. I'm so sorry you lost her."

"Thank you, it was hard."

They were quiet for a few moments and Rose said, "Let me show you where the intruder breached the compound." Robert followed her back through the yard and directly beyond the great picture window.

"Here, see the smashed greens of my tulip bed? He stomped it all down when he came over the fence. The dogs started barking and I saw movement when I shined the light over here. That was terrifying, I'll never forget that feeling."

"I wish I knew why someone would come onto the property knowing you were all here. Usually these kind of incidents take place when no one's home."

"I don't know. But it has me unnerved. I have to turn every light out when I go into a room, it feels like we're being watched."

"Oh, that must be scary for you. We've been watching the area, but there hasn't been anything similar reported."

"Do you think someone is interested in Skyler? I mean because of the kidnapping last March?"

"I'm not sure. I'll go back over the file. You've all been through a lot of bizarre events. I'm also aware that your son-in law Jimmy Conrad is a convict."

"They aren't married, but yes, Jimmy served time for drugs. I've forgiven him, and he's definitely trying very hard to seek retribution. He's been amazing to the kids. We've become a family after all these years. I actually do consider Jimmy part of this family."

"Forgive me, Rose, but is there any chance that the intruder has found you through him?"

"Oh, I just don't know anymore. I'm not sure what to think. I just want us to be safe and secure. I've never felt so scared in my own home. The fear that something will happen to any of them debilitates me."

"We're all keeping an eye out for you. Try not to worry too much."

They heard someone calling, "Grandma? Where are you?"

It was Skyler, coming down the path, Matilda running at her heels.

"Oh, can I come in?" She asked as she reached the gazebo and stepped to the entrance.

"Of course, Sweetheart. We were just talking."

"Carla said to tell you we're all having ice cream sundaes for dessert, if you're interested."

"My favorite. Yes ma'am wouldn't miss that," Chief Leigh exclaimed.

The chief and Rose stood and started toward the house, the child and the dog trailing behind them.

"I sure like your place here, Skyler. It's incredible."

"Thank-you. Grandma takes care of everything. She even takes care of all of us too."

"I can see that she does." He was smiling, completely enchanted with the two ladies escorting him through the garden of fragrant lilies. He was having a great time being here this evening.

There was some romantic chemistry happening in the kitchen. Annie and Jimmy were dishing out the ice cream. As their hands brushed one another, an invisible spark shot through them. They both felt it. Annie pulled her hand away and looked at Jimmy.

"What was that?" she was staring at him, grinning.

"You are electric, woman!" They were both laughing as the kids came in.

"Hey, share. What's so funny?" Bo said.

"Oh, your dad is trying to electrocute me. I just got shocked." Bo was watching them. Here lately, they were grinning at one another a lot, as if they had a secret. It was strange to see, but Bo found himself thinking that maybe, just maybe, his folks could actually be happy together again. Deep in his heart, he knew that they still cared about each other. He was going to talk to Grandma about this soon. He wanted to see if she was seeing what he was.

It was a jovial evening that ended way too early. As the chief was leaving, Rose walked him out. The family stood waving and saying good-bye, before Carla came over and shut the door.

"You go do homework, now," she told Bo and Sky. "I'll take the dogs outside." She swished the two kids up with her hand, gesturing for them to scaddaddle up the stairs. Then she went back to the porch side window and looked out at the two folks talking leisurely. The wheels were turning in her mind as she thought of how those two seemed to suit one another. She grinned and hummed to herself as she made her way into the kitchen. She let the tiny dogs out to take care of their business for the night.

"Jesu, bring the love to my Rosa. Amen." She prayed as she went about the task of cleaning up her kitchen.

Downstairs in the media room, Annie was putting in an old movie. She'd just gotten tucked in to watch it, when Jimmy came in.

"Watcha watching, Toots?" He asked her.

"The Sands of Time," she told him. "It's a long movie, a classic. Watch with me."

"Okay, tell you what, I'll be back after I go up and see if Sky or Bo need any help with their homework, Okay?"

"Sounds good. Oh, and Jimmy?"

"Yea, Toots?"

"You're an amazing father."

"Aw shucks, thanks, that's one of the nicest things you've ever said to me. I love you."

Annie got still for a minute, and then turned to watch him go toward the stairs. He loved her? She shook her head a minute. Jimmy loved her? The movie was already playing, but Annie was somewhere else. Her heart was opening up like a flower and Jimmy was the sun, warming it.

He got shaky. It had just slipped out; he didn't mean to say it so casually. He felt awkward, as if he'd just fallen on his face right in front of her. He was vulnerable. She had the power to crush him right now, and that was making him fidget.

He entered his son's room, after knocking and hearing, "Come in."

"How goes it, my Son?"

"It's just fine. I have to write a paper about my favorite food and read it out loud. It's my public speaking class."

"Do you want to practice on me?"

Bo was laughing at him, "Nah, but thanks, I appreciate the offer. I'm still perfecting it."

"Okay. Hey, Bo, can I ask you a question?"

"Sure Dad, shoot."

"I'm not sure how to say this, I kind of want to ask your mom out on a date. Do you think that would be okay with you? I don't want it to feel funny. I want you to approve I guess."

"Wow, really Dad? That is weird, but it's okay. We are a family already." He felt himself getting emotional. "I love you both, Dad. You're my parents, I want everyone to be happy."

Jimmy was nodding, "I hear you, and I love you all very much. I'm going to go real slow here, I don't want to spook anyone. I guess I've always loved your Mom. There's never been anyone else."

He went over to hug his son and ruffled his hair.

"You really don't mind?" Jimmy asked once more.

"Nope. I really don't."

"Thanks, Bud, you're an amazing guy, you know that?" Bo smiled at his dad. They were both still grinning as he backed out and headed to his baby girl's room.

Skyler was sitting back on some pillows reading a book, when her dad tapped on her door. He pushed it open and said, "Hi there Squirt. What are you up to?"

"Just reading, Dad. What are you up to?"

"I was coming to check on you and see if you need help with your homework or anything. Do you?"

"No. I got it all done."

"Your mom wants to watch some old love story downstairs, I guess I'll go join her."

"You know Dad, she watches you sometimes." Jimmy perked up, alert.

"What do you mean, Munchkin?"

"I've seen her. Like when you leave, she goes to the window and watches you walk all the way and get into the car. She watches."

"Okay. Well I guess that's fine, I don't mind. Do you think she misses me when I'm gone?" He was holding his breath. He didn't want to bait Sky, he just needed her take.

"Dad, do you miss her when you leave to go to work?"

"Yes, I missed your mom for a long, long time. She wrote me letters when I got sent away for drugs, but I guess she grew to forget me after a while. I understood…I was paying a price and not having her was part of the payment. Not having you was part of it too."

"We all get to be together now, right Dad?"

"Yes, Munchkin, we do. I love you."

"I love you too, Dad. Now go watch a movie with mom and tell her you missed her."

"Okay, I will. Goodnight, Sweetheart."

"Goodnight, Daddy." He stepped over and bent down to give her a peck on her soft cheek, then softly closed the door on his way out. He was grinning to himself thinking of what his kids had just said to him. They were okay with him being with their mom again. He felt like skipping as he headed back toward the lower levels of the house, where Annie waited.

He was feeling pretty humble these days. God was being so good to him. His kids were growing closer to him every day and Annie? He loved Annie. That was a revelation that hit him right in the heart. He loved her very much.

On the other side of the house, Rose was gathering her things for a bath. She got it all laid out and headed through the halls to find the kids, and tell them goodnight. She went in and kissed Bo, then Sky and headed down to hug Annie.

As she went down a few stairs, it occurred to her that Annie and Jimmy were watching a movie. The lights were dimmed and their heads were very close together. Rose was four steps from the bottom, when she had an epiphany. These two loved each other. They had been apart for almost nine years. The separation had not led them to anywhere, but right back here where they started.

She backed up slowly, deciding not to interrupt. As she traveled back to her quarters, she was pondering on the scene, and if in fact it meant something was happening between them. It would be perfectly natural for Jimmy and Annie to fall back in love.

Back in town, a man was taking a trip down memory lane. He talked to the portrait of Ava Leigh, willing her to change expression and give him some sign that he was not alone.

"I miss you, Honey. I still make horrible coffee and burn toast. Why did yours always taste so perfect? I met a lady, dear. She's a real fine Christian woman. I know it's not news to you, you probably see everything. Do you think I have any chance of making a woman want to be around me? I know I'm a little over weight, and my muscles are not all firm like they used to be, but Honey, it sure was nice to just hear a lady laugh. I guess I'll go to bed now. Goodnight, Ava."

Every once in a while, he talked to her all night long, but he was tired now. Tired of the echo in the house, and his words bouncing back to him, unanswered and unacknowledged. He missed his wife in more ways than anyone could ever imagine. He missed the touch of her hand on his hair and he missed the look she gave him if he brought her a gift. Most of all he missed just knowing she was waiting for him when he came home.

Robert cried that night. She'd been gone for almost two years, but the grief was still heavy on his heart. He knew he was starting to heal though. He smelled flowers and women's perfume, and it made him smile. Before, just after she passed, those things made him ache inside with longing.

Rose had invited him to the worship service at her church. He told her he would try to pop in this Sunday. Robert believed in God, always had, but ever since Ava passed away, he couldn't think about church. He needed to heal the open wound on his heart his own way.

The morning air was crisp, it had rained just before he set out. Now, the sun was beating down on the moist pavement. Robert walked a lot through town, seeing things up close and personal. As he traveled in the direction of Rivers Oak Church, he caught glimpses of himself in storefront reflections. Robert wore a suit today and he felt quite dapper. He'd gotten a new haircut as well, taking extra time this morning on his shave.

The rain was long gone and his mood lifted with each block that he got closer to her. His feelings for Rose were warm, and he respected her more than any woman he knew right now. There was a tiny hole in the dam he'd built around his emotions. Thoughts of her were bringing forth sunlight and the rays were shining through.

The church was very large, and the parking lot was full. People came from miles away to attend. Rose was amazingly gifted at speaking, possessing a rare ability to reach straight into the hearts of her followers. They returned again and again. The faces shifted and grew, seeming to multiply every Sunday.

She saw him as he wound his way forward. He was trying to sit front and center, so he could see and hear every word.

She smiled out at him. It pleased her that he'd come. She felt his eyes on her and found her self tingle with awareness. That was unexpected. She was starting to come to the realization that this man affected her.

The service had begun. Today, her sermon was about the lost and wandering. As the worship music died down and the lector took her seat, Rose began,

"My friends, have you ever lost your child in a busy crowd? I have. It was at an amusement park. One minute she was there and the next she was gone. I finally found her in a tented area, where a sign read: Lost Parents. The humor of the tilted sign was lost on me, I was frantic. When Annie saw me, she ran to me and screamed, "Mom!" My child knew me, and was happy that I found her. We were reunited, it was wonderful. So, imagine you live your life denying our Father. You never acknowledge Him or seek Him. In essence you are like the lost child in an amusement park. When it's closing, you wander around seeking your parent, or your companion, you feel lost. I need you to hear what I'm saying to you now. When you're dying… there is a time that you are crossing over, when you are almost on the other side. Remember the park has closed, suddenly, there He is. Your Father is there to get you. It's time to go. He's your Father and you know Him. You are so elated to see Him because you've been lost. He reaches out His hand to you and you take it. Then, you go with Him. You see my friends, we know our Father. When He reveals himself to us, and beckons, we know Him and we go because He is God. He takes us home."

"Pray with me now, for all of the lost: The people living behind steel bars or imprisoned by drugs or prostitution, the ones addicted to pornography or heroin. It doesn't matter what booth we are in, or what game we are playing, it is a carnival. The world leads us away from the will of our Father. He simply wants us to know Him and to choose Him. Lord, we ask that You shine that warm light on our face. With the rising and the setting of the sun, show us Your majesty. May we know that You are there, waiting patiently for us to choose to leave the roller coaster ride for a while, and just walk with You and toward You, where You wait. Make us see that we are Your children and we are lost. We ask in Jesus' name. Amen."

Robert held his breath. She was spectacular. He was touched deeply by her message, and made a decision to buy and read her books.

As the music died down, people started moving toward the door. Robert just sat there in his seat, waiting for her. She was at the great double doors, touching, hugging, kissing and sharing everything with the people who came here today.

Robert had nothing but time. A pager was vibrating on his hip and he ignored it. The station knew he was in church. There were several people capable of handling ninety-nine percent of the issues that needed to be addressed at the station. People break the law 24/7. There's no day of rest for the chief, never a 'closed' day at the office. Sundays are just another day, but he turned the pager off.

Fifteen minutes passed by, and he still sat quietly, waiting and watching. Finally, she excused herself from the throngs and came toward him, sliding into the pew. She smiled at him and said, "Thanks for coming. You know, I don't think I've ever sat here before." She felt his side, and it was warm. She liked it.

Robert felt like a new man: relaxed, open, human. Her message made him feel safe. As he took in the great arched walls, and gentle murmurs of happy people reverberating around the room, he was thinking to himself, *I like it here.*

"You were wonderful. I feel privileged to be your friend." He looked at her. She was so close to him and he felt such a connection. It was a feeling he needed. He wanted it to continue.

"Can I take you to dinner later?"

"Oh, I suppose I could work it into my schedule."

"I have a special place I like to go; nothing fancy, but the food is excellent and I always get a good table."

"I can be ready at six. How's that?"

"Perfect. I'll be there at six sharp milady."

Rose told him she had to talk to a few people, and make a few plans for some upcoming events. She reached out and took his hand, looking him in the eye.

"I'm so glad you came today. It's so good to see you. I look forward to this evening."

"Me too. Have a great day Rose, see you tonight." She nodded her head at him, grinned and left him there, smiling.

If the people at the station could see him now, they wouldn't recognize him. He hadn't worn a suit since he buried his wife. This was a happier occasion. He would be coming back to the church again soon, maybe even next week.

As he walked to his car he saw Rose's family outside. They were chatting with some folks and gave him a wave.

"Hi, Chief," yelled Bo. "Good to see you."

"Good to see you all. Have a great day."

Bo and Jimmy looked at each other, and Bo said, "Dad, I think he likes Grandma."

"Oh I know he does, Bo. I know for sure he does."

Of course they all approved. The chief was a great guy.

15

Finding Tina

Fall was coming, and the nights had grown cold. Rose and Robert were enjoying a quiet evening at his home in front of the fireplace. She sipped on a cup of chamomile tea, while Robert enjoyed a glass of Merlot. He talked briefly about Ava, while showing Rose the house. She sensed his loneliness as they gazed at portraits lining the wall. She watched him as he folded the small towel and tidied up the kitchen. He told her it took a while, but he'd adjusted to being a widower.

It was romantic to be here. Rose loved the old Victorian farmhouse with its white picket fence. There was something so cozy and safe being in his home. No one would dare disturb his property.

She was telling him about Annie's abduction. It was completely unbelievable, but he knew it was true. He just sat there shaking his head and nodding, allowing her to share with him all of the sheer panic she felt. As she told Robert about what the medium said, he was fascinated.

"I wish we had someone like her here on the force to help us. I would find answers to several mysteries and maybe even solve some cases. Sometimes one little detail can help. We have a lead on a suspect that we believe might be involved in the abduction of Tina Mason, who was taken from her yard over three weeks ago."

"Oh my, that poor girl! You know, we held a candlelight prayer vigil for her. God, I pray she's still alive, Robert."

"I do too. If we could just locate the suspect, but, it seems like he's gone off the grid. We found his brother, but that's where the trail goes cold."

"You know, I can call Emily. She lives in Columbia. Would you like to meet her?"

"I would be very interested in meeting her Rose. If you say she is the real deal, I believe you. If she could help us in the Mason case, I'd be very grateful."

"I'll contact her tomorrow."

"Thanks Rose, I really appreciate any small lead here. We've hit a brick wall."

"No problem. She's a delightful young woman. I look forward to seeing her again as well."

It was getting late. Rose gathered her sweater and went toward the door.

Robert touched her hand and when she didn't pull away, he held it a moment.

"I've really enjoyed our evening, Rose. Thank you for allowing me to take you out to dinner tonight."

"Thank you. I haven't been out like that with anyone in a very long time. I enjoyed your company very much. If you don't mind, I'd love to go back to Sophia's to eat again sometime. I found the ambience simply lovely."

Robert smiled, and Rose found herself looking at his mouth. It was soft and sweet looking. She turned a rosy color as she realized he was studying her, while she studied him. They grinned, sharing the mutual attraction.

"I guess I'll talk to you later, Robert. Goodnight."

He felt a churning in his stomach at the thought of not holding her close to him. He tried to fight it, but it was too strong. He reached out and gently brought her to his chest, holding her there. After a few seconds, he spoke.

"I'd like to see you again soon. Can I call you tomorrow evening?"

Rose smiled. "Of course, I'd say 7 PM would be suitable. I'll look forward to your call." She lost contact then, as she stepped off the porch and turned to go down the path.

"Sleep well," he called out to her.

"You too. Talk to you tomorrow."

It had been so sweet to just be with her. She was unlike anyone in this entire world; of that, he was certain. As he turned to go into the quiet house, he felt like there was something exciting and wonderful to look forward to now. His step was lighter as he went through the house and into the kitchen to tidy up. He felt happy, and as he picked up the teacup that had her light lipstick on the rim, it occurred to him that he was feeling different. Something was changing; a dark shadow was slowly lifting.

Rose was having a lovely day. She was looking forward to fall. The trees were turning brilliant orange and magenta and there was a crackle in the air. October was her favorite month. She and Annie decorated the porch with pumpkins and great pots of chrysanthemums. The little dogs felt the brisk mood as well and ran around and around the hedgerows, playing catch.

Emily Stone was coming on Friday. Rose invited her to stay in the guesthouse near the lake while she was in town. She graciously accepted, so the family was excited. They were all in awe of her. Everyone was looking forward to having her here.

Robert was preparing a presentation of the Tina Mason case to Emily. He was trying to keep an open mind about paranormal premonitions. If God had created us all unique and different, then who was to say that some people didn't have special sight? He'd seen for himself what Skyler had been blessed with. It was something that he kept quiet about, though. His relationship with Rose put everything into a new perspective. He believed her, without question, and he wanted to protect them all.

Carla, Annie, and Skyler cleaned the house from top to bottom. It was exciting to be having a guest. Carla was a little concerned about mediums. She was Catholic and she'd been brought up to believe that sighted people were open to bad spirits. Her concern was that Emily would bring a bad spirit into the house. Carla was superstitious. Skyler laughed at her.

"Carla, you are so funny. Emily is just as normal as I am. She just sees things that other people can't. Don't be afraid of her. Just remember that she's like me; not scary, just different."

"Okay Nina, I will try not to be scared of her, but I'm still keeping my lucky rabbit foot nearby."

Skyler was laughing. "Okay. I'm sure that it'll keep the bad juju spirits away."

They both laughed together, continuing the polishing of the wooden railings that graced the main staircase leading to the upper levels of the house.

There were no more incidences with the prowler. The family was feeling better these days and the security system had been upgraded and tested. The chief patrolled the winding country road that lead to the England compound almost daily. He kept his eyes peeled to any strange license plates in town as well. One could never be too vigilant.

It was Friday afternoon when Emily arrived. Carla and Rose got her all settled in. She was asked to come up to the house as soon as she was freshened up, they would be having a small party this evening to celebrate. As soon as the kids got home from school, they were told to finish their homework so they were free to just hang out with the family. Robert was set to arrive soon as well.

Everyone was gathered around the breakfast bar having cheese and crackers when the doorbell rang. Carla brought Robert in, and Rose made introductions. Emily and Robert shook hands and exchanged pleasantries.

"I certainly have heard amazing things about you, Ms. Stone."

"Oh please, call me Emily."

"Okay, and you can call me Robert."

"So nice to be here…."

Emily had just barely let go of his hand, and was already picking up something extraordinary about him. She felt a presence very close to him. She felt like it was his wife. Yes, it was his wife, and she was definitely here, right behind him one minute, and in front of him the next.

Rose was watching, and realized something was going on.

"What is it, Emily? Your face has gone stiff. What's happening?"

"It's hard, I'm being barraged right now by the spirit of someone who has passed. She is very protective of the chief, and I feel that she is worried about me being here with him. I'm hearing the name, "Robbie.""

They all looked at the chief as he turned ashen white.

Emily smiled then, "Robert, your wife is passed, correct?"

"Yes, almost two years ago this December. Why? What are you seeing?"

"She's here. She stays near you, hovering around, protecting you. She's a guardian angel for you here."

Robert put his hands up to his face and said, "Oh my God." He was starting to tear up. He wasn't expecting this. It was uncanny.

"It doesn't surprise me that you're sensing Ava. We were together for 31 years. She was a good woman and a great wife. She waited up for me so many times, worrying when I was late. She always did call me Robbie. It doesn't surprise me at all that she's here."

Emily explained. "She died at peace. I'm feeling that. She just wanted to let me know that she's right here with us. Strong spirits will do that; make their presence known immediately. It's something most people go through life never knowing, that a loved one is with them in spirit. A lot of people suppress and deny the signs when they're there."

"I hear knocking sometimes." Robert stated.

They had all taken a seat, or just found a place to lean. It was a conversation that sucked them all in, as they hung on every word spoken.

Robert resumed his story. "I thought for sure someone was at the door, but when I opened it, there was no one. It has happened twice. Once, it was my birthday, and I was listening to the radio and making a Reuben sandwich. I heard loud knocking four feet away by the back door. I went out side and walked all the way around the house but there wasn't anyone around."

"That is a very common communicative tool." Emily told him. "I have heard that several times before. Do you remember how many knocks you heard?"

"Yes. Exactly three distinct knocks. I even looked at the door because it came from there."

"I have a theory. It involves the amount of knocks correlating to the message. Chief, I feel like the message might have been, *Happy Birthday Robbie.*"

"Yes, I suppose it could've been."

Robert was shaking his head. Unbelievable. No one would believe that in the first ten minutes of meeting this clairvoyant she told him Ava was here with him. It was a feeling unlike anything he'd ever experienced. He wanted to cry, but there was too much to do. His goal was to find a little girl and he wanted to keep that uppermost in his mind.

The family sat down to eat a delicious Mexican feast, prepared lovingly by Carla.

Annie and Jimmy sat across from Bo and Skyler, who were kicking them and pretending they had no idea who was behind it. The evening was promising to be filled with lots of laughter as well as intrigue.

"Emily, I was hoping you could come with me to the location of the abduction case I told you about. We have very little to go on, except an eyewitness that saw a black Mazda zooming away from the site. We found a match and have questioned the owner of the vehicle, but he has disappeared. I have been increasingly frustrated about this case." Robert wasn't sure how to proceed, but he wanted to take her there, to the last place Tina Mason had been.

"Of course. Rose has filled me in on a few details. What time would be good for you, Chief?"

"How about 10 AM, and if you would like, we could take it into lunch. I know a few good spots and I always get a great table."

He looked at Rose and winked. She was his favorite person to squire around, but tomorrow he was going to be in the presence of a very unique young woman. He hoped Ava approved. He knew one thing: if Emily Stone could help him solve this case, he would be forever in her debt.

That night as he wound his way down and out to the rambling Victorian he'd shared with Ava, he felt her. She'd never really left him. He knew it. Every time he talked to her, he knew she was there. Sometimes he would awaken from a deep sleep and a light would be on in the house. He never left lights on, and he would go turn it off, but he thought to himself that she always loved her lamps and lights.

Ava had a reading chair with a special lamp that shined on her page, but she also had indirect lamps that she liked to have on if she was watching television. There was one she loved best. Very delicate, it sits on an antique table in the corner near the window. He would see it burning long after she retired to bed, a beacon for him that she was waiting for him to get home before she would turn the lights out.

There were two separate times since she passed, that he woke up to a light blazing. He'd simply discounted it to a shaky chain or a faulty lever. What was significant to him was the third time. He was fully awake when he pulled into the drive to see the small lamp lit. That had messed with his mind. That, was the lamp she turned on for him.

He was ready to open his mind. Little Skyler had pried it open with her visions, but now he was wide open to the premonitions of Emily. Before he pulled out of his driveway this morning, he bowed his head and said a prayer.

"God, please allow this young woman to see what happened to Tina. We need you to guide us, Lord. We need to find Herman Shores. We need to bring this little girl home."

He stayed that way a moment longer than usual, reiterating that he was serious about his prayer. Then he put the cruiser in reverse, and headed in the direction of the unknown, hopeful.

She stood very still, as she studied the last known place Tina Mason had been. Emily was focused on the play area in the side yard. Tina would swing every day after school, and run around with her dog. Her mother had a clear view of the yard, and watched vigilantly from the kitchen window. That day, the clothes dryer had gone off, and she had stepped into the adjoining hall, to gather the laundry for folding. Her mind was on the next chore, making grilled cheese sandwiches for lunch.

One minute Tina was there and four minutes later, she was gone. A lady mail carrier had seen one vehicle in the area around that time. She looked at pictures and pointed to the make and model that matched. It was a black Mazda, 2000 to 2004. It was older, that was all she could tell. She saw a man with a grayish stocking cap driving. No other passengers that she could detect. It was a split second observation, but it was all they had to go on.

Missouri DMV found three black Mazda's registered in the county that fit the description. One was in a salvage yard; one was owned and driven by Doris Meyer, who was a suburban mother of two, and a man named Herman Shores owned the third one.

The police went to the address on file and questioned him for thirty minutes. He stated he was working at the time of the abduction, and then changed his story. He told them he was at a park, eating lunch in his car near the street where she was taken. It didn't add up, and there was no corroborating information to back up his version of the timeline.

Mr. Shores was placed at the top of their suspect list. He had ultimately failed to give a credible alibi as to his whereabouts during the time the child was taken. He was told to stay in the area and remain available for further questioning. That was over two weeks ago. Mr. Shores had disappeared and his family stated they had no clue where he'd gone.

Emily told Robert she would enter into a trance and try to bring forth some images they could use. He was asked not to interrupt or allow anyone near her.

As she held Tina's favorite doll, the images were gathering quickly in her mind. The child was running around her, laughing, jumping and shouting. Emily felt the images grow sharper, and she turned her head toward the street.

Her eyes were being drawn to a man. His shadow was there first, fleetingly, because in the instant his shadow appeared, she felt malevolence. He was roughly grabbing her, and Emily flinched as she experienced what little Tina had endured. She was lifted and quickly carried away from her swing set. She cried out once, "Mom!" but already, the sky was flying by above her, as she looked at the man's head in the gray hat. He'd pushed her down into the back seat floorboard.

She was seeing what the child went through, and salty tears flowed as she felt him and his intentions. He was not normal, his perverted thoughts flew through Emily's mind and she shook her head to dispel images that were of a dark nature. Then the pictures started flashing quickly. She was deep in a trance, and in it, she was being shown everything they needed to know.

She was with Tina in the car, watching her cry for her mother. Finally they came to a stop. The man carried the child up the rickety stairs and in, shutting the door firmly behind him. Then she concentrated some more and saw Tina sleeping in a dark room.

Emily opened her eyes. They were all there...watching her. She gathered herself a moment, trying to clear her mind of the evil thoughts she'd been exposed to, focusing on the information she'd gleaned. She turned and walked over to where the chief stood.

"He has her. He's in a trailer south of here. I see a large corn silo and a big red barn. There's a huge tornado warning antennae on his east side. The car is around back. She's inside and he's been keeping her locked in a room. He's also been keeping her very sleepy."

Robert wasted no time. He called the National Weather Station and stated who he was. He asked for a digital map of every tornado antennae system in the county, as well as the counties south of Franklin. He went back to Emily.

"Is she hurt, Emily? Can you tell me if we're going to need an ambulance?"

"She's dehydrated and drugged. Yes, he's hurt her and abused her. She's alive, though. He doesn't want to commit murder."

The investigation was spinning. As the information came in, the squads were given a map and told to disperse immediately. They kept it from the press, not wanting to spook Herman. Keeping the element of surprise was imperative.

Two hours from the time Emily Stone spoke of the trailer, it was located. The child was found and rushed to the hospital. Robert did something he'd prayed for weeks to be able to do: he called her family.

She was missing for 24 days. In the hands of a pedophile, she'd been molested repeatedly. Now, she was being treated at the Children's Hospital. Her condition was improving rapidly with fluids and the tearful reunion with her mother and father.

Chief Leigh and Emily were quietly speaking to the family when Rose arrived. She told them she would be in the Chapel. She was praying for the family and the child. The ordeal had taken a horrific toll on them all, but God had delivered Tina back to her parents, and Rose needed to give Him praise.

She was kneeling in the front pew when she felt a presence beside her. It was Robert; he'd come to join her in giving thanks. It was a miracle the child was found alive. He was humbled this day. For so many things, he was grateful.

The Mason family made a statement to the press. They thanked first Ms. Emily Stone, and vowed they would forever be indebted to her. Then they thanked the Eureka Police Department for their tenacity in searching every crevice to find Tina. Finally, as the camera zoomed into their emotional press conference, they thanked Rose England, for bringing her friend Emily Stone to help them find their little girl.

"I was a skeptic about psychics," said Mr. Mason to the gathered cameras. "Now, I realize there are miracles and God does answer prayers, through people like psychics. I am now a believer! I want to thank Ms. Stone from the bottom of my heart. We are so incredibly grateful for her extraordinary gift. Thank you all for your continued prayers as well, my family and I are still in need of them."

Tina Mason survived and thrived. Her family eventually moved away from the house and the yard that held so much sadness. There remained an unbendable connection to Rose, the chief and his staff. Every year during the holidays, a smattering of Christmas cards arrived, thanking them all over and over again, for helping to find and bring their baby girl home.

16
Change of Seasons

The leaves were completely off the trees now as winter set in. It was the week before Christmas and things had returned to normal around the house. The kids were happy to have both parents with them.

Bo was driving the Rover to his job and to school now. He brought a girl home one day to meet everyone. Her name was Cindy and they were inseparable. They watched movies, and went out four-wheeling around the property. Rose and Annie approved wholeheartedly.

Annie had a job in town. She worked at a boutique, and she loved it. It occurred to her that she could dress like a lady for once in her life. She'd never cared about clothes that much, but now she dressed all of her customers. She was happier than she'd ever been in her life.

This Christmas was going to be extremely special. They planned a quiet evening at home with a gift exchange and Annie had shopped every day. Robert and Jimmy had brought the Christmas tree in, which was enormous. Mountains of gifts piled up both walls behind it, surrounding it with glittering packages.

Robert was a different man these days. Everyone at the station commented on his happy glow. The same man that had holed up at home for two years, letting his life shrivel up around him, had transformed into a sociable gentleman. He had a surprise for Rose this year.

Jimmy was content for the first time in his life as well. He had been out of the joint for almost a year. He'd have to do something really amazing to celebrate that anniversary, and hopefully he'd be with Annie. He wanted to take her somewhere special, somewhere neither of them had ever been. He wanted to tell her he loved her.

It was December 22nd. The family was going to Tilles Park this evening to see Christmas lights. Everyone piled into the Escalade with Carla chauffeuring. They snuggled under blankets and chattered about what they wanted for Christmas.

Skyler had her head on Jimmy's shoulder and was feeling content. The low vibration in his chest as he spoke and the murmur of voices was lulling her to sleep.

Something was happening all of the sudden. There was a car flying in the air and it was heading straight toward them. Skyler sat straight up and grabbed Carla by the shoulder.

"Carla, pull over!"

"What are you talking about Nina?"

"It's coming fast and it's coming at us. Pull over now Carla!"

Carla was on the highway, but she put on her turn signal and pulled to the shoulder. She put on her emergency flashers and everyone was quiet.

"Are we going to be okay, Ms. Sky?" she asked. This was scaring her. She'd never been involved in an accident and she didn't particularly want to continue driving at all if Skyler saw one coming at her.

"Mr. Jimmy, you take the wheel now, please?" she asked.

"Just a minute, Carla, wait." Skyler said softly, while chewing her nails with worry.

They all just sat there…waiting.

Suddenly a mile ahead they saw it. A car was literally flying through the air coming from the other side of the highway and it crashed hard and bounced onto its side.

"Oh my God!" Jimmy cried. He and Bo were in the backseat and they told Carla to get over to the crash site. They wanted to see if they could help. Rose was in the front seat dialing 911.

"We are at Ladue Road, exit 141. Please hurry, it doesn't look good."

The Escalade was pulled onto the shoulder and people were stopped every direction, running toward the wreck. Annie, Rose, Carla, and Skyler stayed in the Escalade, praying for the people to live.

The car was lying on the driver's side. Both passengers were unresponsive. Jimmy had run over to the vehicle and climbed up, trying to get the door open to help get the passenger out. Bo was looking into the smashed windshield at a younger man's face. He didn't see movement.

"Help me, Bo! Grab him from under his arms and help me lift." Jimmy was determined to help.

Four minutes later, they were able to bring the elderly passenger out of the vehicle and lay him down. He was bleeding from the head, but was breathing. As the EMS workers reached them, they requested that folks back up and give them room to work. It didn't look good for the driver.

Jimmy went back to the car, and told them he wasn't sure of the condition of the men. The family was in a somber mood and decided to make a night of it. They turned around and traveled home. The trip to see Christmas lights palled when they realized a man had probably lost his life tonight.

That evening at 9 PM the wreck was being covered on the news. The man in the driver's side had passed away. The elderly gentleman was in a coma, and critical, but they were hopeful that his injuries were not fatal. Once again, Skyler had protected them from harm. If they were one mile farther down the highway, they all could have been killed tonight.

Rose was telling Robert all about it on the telephone.

"It happened so fast, Robert. One minute we're all talking and she's just napping, then all of a sudden we are stopped and watching this horrific scene. It is beyond bizarre."

"Oh Rose, I'm so glad you're all okay. I can't lose you."

"You're so silly, I'm not going anywhere. Listen, I want you to come for dinner on Christmas Eve. Six o'clock sharp, what do you say?"

"Well I don't have any better offers. I guess I'll accept. What can I bring?"

"Just your big old self and maybe a bottle of that Malbac I like, if you don't mind."

"You got it Rose. Tonight I'm going to say a special prayer and I'm going to thank your grandma, Marie. She's saved you from death a couple of times now through your granddaughter. It's an amazing thing, just amazing."

"Yes, it is something alright. We are reeling from the experience. I can't go to that place in my mind where we could have been completely crushed by that car. I still wonder what happened."

"I do too. Maybe the accident report will tell us eventually why it happened. For now, I'm just grateful you weren't in the path of it. It's a miracle."

"Yes, I guess it is. Goodnight Robert."

"Goodnight Rose, sleep well."

She smiled as she disconnected from him. They were becoming an item.

The following Sunday, Rose gathered her family and headed to church. It was a Christmas service and they were all dressed up. She watched from her seat on the raised dais as they all filed into the pews and got seated.

The choir stood and performed "Silent Night" and Rose knew this was a special Christmas for her. She continued to gaze lovingly at her kids, all of them, and she was proud. Then, her eyes fell on him as he came closer to her family and they all scooted over to allow him in, next to them.

Rose knew her life was changing. She'd never felt a need for a man in her life, content with her chosen vocation, her mate was her pulpit, and her heart was with her church family. That was changing now.

The farmhouse was a place that drew her. She and Robert would sit out on the porch watching the sky darken and sharing companionship. He moved her just by a touch or a word. Rose was deeply in love, and that was a brand new development. She would have to discuss it soon with her family.

Something extraordinary happened that evening after a huge turkey dinner. As the red candles glittered and the Christmas tree shimmered, the family was exchanging gifts in the warm family room downstairs.

It was nearing the end, and everyone was winding down from the excitement. The fire crackled and the family was feeling full from the spirit of giving, when Robert spoke up. All eyes turned to him, and he reddened visibly. His hands started to sweat.

"I have something for you, Rose." He stood and moved closer to where she sat perched in her favorite chair. Robert knelt down in front of her and smiled at the confused expression she gave him.

"From the first time I met you, I felt the need to be near you. It was at the station, and you were crying for Skyler. Rose, I think I fell in love with you instantly." He dug into his jacket and pulled out a tiny box, and opened it. Then, he presented it to Rose.

"I love you. You've made my life wonderful again, and it would make me the happiest man in the world, if you would be my wife, Rose Marie England."

The room was silent for a second, and Rose looked at the dear faces surrounding her. Then she touched the cross that hung around her neck, looked at the man who bore his love for her in his eyes, and knew what her answer would be.

"Yes. Yes, I will be your wife!"

The room erupted with congratulations. Annie couldn't control it any longer as she loudly, but happily, cried into her tissue. Everyone had witnessed the event, and they were moved to tears. They saw Rose grab hold of Robert as the two embraced, and held one another. Jimmy grabbed Annie and hugged her, and the kids hugged Rose and Robert in turn. They'd just shared a very personal moment and it left them all raw with emotion.

Robert and Rose excused themselves to go into the front room. They sat on the sofa as he murmured how happy she had made him. She was reveling in the feel of his chest, hard and solid. In all of her days, she'd never felt so warm, protected and loved. It was truly a gift from God, a special gift He had for her.

The couple made arrangements for a simple country wedding in the spring, right on the compound. As the winter snows melted, and the crocuses made their appearance, that day arrived. Rose asked her good friend Pastor Gloria Jean to officiate. The family and a few close friends gathered in the chairs assembled.

Robert was a sight to behold as he stood waiting for Rose to appear. Everyone watched, as this hulking man held his emotions in check. He would not succeed, for as his bride approached him, he openly cried, and she as well. The vows were spoken and rings exchanged. Rose, was now Mrs. Robert Leigh.

The couple decided that Rose would reside mostly at the farmhouse with Robert. The compound would still be home for Annie, Jimmy, Bo, and Skyler, but Carla was torn. The time for her to be closer to her own daughter was approaching, as there was a grandchild now. It was one of the hardest decisions she had to make, but she ultimately decided to move to Chicago, Illinois. Her daughter Angelina, and her 4-year-old grandson Bennie were her number one priority now.

Skyler's visions continued to awaken her for several years. She tried to remain anonymous with her warnings, but there were times when people got wind of what was happening. For some reason, the visions seemed to be focused on Robert a lot.

He was planning to travel out to a rural area one Tuesday morning, to arrest some men in an alleged theft ring. The planning had been in progress for a week. Robert and seven officers were to make up the team. The surveillance showed a very savvy group, some convicts, and some just plain mean men; they were fully armed.

Roberts's team laid out precise plans the evening before. It was a surprise raid and the timing was crucial. He'd slept at the station, ready to act, ready to engage. The search warrant was already in his possession. At 4 AM, the team was set to move on the rural outpost.

Skyler woke up that morning at 3:15 AM, with a vision of Robert's car on fire. She called him immediately. When he heard her voice, he knew he had to take heed to what she had to tell him.

The HAZMAT team was called in to search the entire lot, and every vehicle. A small, crude, deadly handmade bomb was discovered under the left front tire of the chief's police cruiser.

The questions came. They wanted to know how she knew the bomb was there. Robert told them it would be explained after the mission was complete. They needed to stay on task.

The early morning siege on the rural St. Clair property netted the Chief and his team five suspects. It was a success, and as they all came together several hours later after booking, the Chief called them into the main conference room for a meeting.

"I want to commend each and every one of you for your diligence in fighting for the safety of the community. Day in and day out, it'll always be good guys against bad. Today some very valuable merchandise will be returned to the good people here. Family, neighbors and friends count on us to do what we did this morning. I'm extremely proud of all of you. You make me look good."

Rhonda was in the back of the room by the door, listening to the Chief.

"Who tipped you off this morning Chief? How'd you know about the explosive devise?" She knew it had something to do with Skyler Conrad. She wondered if he'd actually say her name.

Robert sat palming his goatee. He would never reveal his source. He smiled and gave her a small nibble, enough to satisfy her for now.

"Rhonda, There's a really special lady in my life. She's in possession of a very rare psychic gift. I'm going to protect her anonymity, but you can be sure of one thing. I trust her and I will always take anything she tells me seriously, no questions asked."

There was a handful in the room that knew exactly who he was referring to. They had answered calls to the compound. Officers Hodges and Alan, exchanged glances with Rhonda. The little girl they'd met six years ago was still having her sleepy visions in the hills.

No one ever bothered the family, but there was talk in the town.

Skyler was still a member of the church and she was well known. Those who knew her grandmother, and her parents Jimmy and Annie, also knew there was something special about Skyler. She would stay away from public gatherings, choosing to seek out her room and a good book. She was sheltered at home in the house in the hills, and she would stay within its walls as much as possible.

Bo joined the U.S. Marines when he turned 22, and left home to seek his own destiny. He left Cindy behind and the couple made a pact to wait for one another.

The day he was leaving, his father shook his hand and told him to watch his back. Then, on impulse, he grabbed his son and hugged him tight.

"I love you, Bo. Never forget where home is."

"I won't, Dad. I love you, too."

Annie was waiting by the car, chewing her fingernails.

"Do you have everything sweetheart?" she asked her son. She felt like she was going to bust out crying as soon as he drove away. It was one of the worst feelings in her life, with the exception of when Skyler was taken.

Now, Skyler was standing near her brother, waiting for him to turn to her. He didn't want to prolong the good-byes. He'd said goodbye to his grandmother and Robert last night.

"I'm going to miss you, Bo." She was sixteen now. Her hair was long and flowed down her back. He could barely look at her without turning into mush; her bright eyes were filling with tears. His sister meant everything to him, always had.

"I'll be back in six months Sky, now don't make this hard for me. I'm not going to cry!"

"Okay. I'll just crack some jokes. You know they're going to shave your head like a fat shiny egg." She was grinning at him and suddenly it was easier.

"Listen, squirt. Stay out of trouble, and if you drive the Rover, remember the clutch sticks. Also, you better train Matilda to sit and stay, cause you know she follows you everywhere and she can fit under the gate. I watched her go down and under it the last time you guys took off on your driving lesson."

Skyler started laughing. "Yea, I know, she's a little shadow."

She got serious then and went in for a bear hug.

"I love you the best out of anybody, Bo. Will you write me a letter, or call me sometime?"

"Of course, squirt, soon as I got something to tell you, I'll try and call. See you soon, love you."

He hugged his mother once more, telling her he loved her. Right before he threw the car into drive, he blew a kiss at his sister and said, "I love you Squirt," and then he drove off. They watched until his taillights were out of sight.

Jimmy looked at the sad faces of Skyler and Annie. Annie went toward the house, while Skyler went to her dad for a hug.

"Come on, he'll be home soon. Let's go in and get some ice cream. I'll race you."

Skyler swiped at the tears on her cheeks, and smiled at her dad. "It's on." They ran all the way to the door and went inside, where Annie was already getting out the bowls.

17
The Legacy

In the next couple of years, more change was coming to the family. Some of the change was not good. Rose had been diagnosed with breast cancer. She fought and prayed for several months, but it was terminal. She was dying.

Her glowing disposition would not allow for despair. She told everyone that she knew exactly where she was going, and it was not a place full of sadness. She knew she would be a guardian angel for them, and she wanted them to prepare themselves to continue life without her in it.

Jimmy and Annie had started to lector at church, taking over some of the very important leadership roles. Last year, they were baptized together. The Reverend Gloria Jean officiated the Baptism ceremony. Rose had happily handed over the reigns to her, with her blessing.

The music was playing and the congregation turned their faces up to a golden-framed window, holding a pool of water. The Reverend entered the sacred space first. Annie stepped into the view of the parishioners and was gathered by the elbow and guided into the pool where the Reverend prayed over her. Her head was gently submerged into the warm fragrant water.

Jimmy looked on from the side. He had tears flowing down his face unchecked. He was experiencing something long overdue. He needed this. After Annie was clear of the water, he went forward, helping her into the tiny dressing area beyond the window. It was his turn now, and like a tiny child he reached for the reverend's hand as she guided him to the place where he would receive Holy Baptism.

Rose sat watching from the pew with the kids and Robert. She was so proud and grateful. Later in the year, both Jimmy and Annie made a decision to become ordained. They were Assistant Pastors to Reverend Gloria. It had become harder and harder for Rose to attend the service, but she gathered up all of her strength and went every week.

Today Jimmy was giving a testimony. They were all there in church. Bo, his girlfriend Cindy, Skyler, Rose, Robert and Annie.

He was nervous. Bo, who stood beside the stage with his dad, put his hand on Jimmy's shoulder.

"You got this, Dad."

That was all it took, as Jimmy looked at his son he said, "Yea, you're right. I got this."

As Jimmy took to the pulpit, his eyes fell on the woman in the pew before him. Not the one who gave him two children, but the one who restored his soul to him. Rose gave him his pride back, gave him unconditional love and showed him what grace truly meant.

He took a deep breath, said a silent prayer and started to speak:

"I was a drug addict. I had two little kids and a good woman, but I chose to do drugs. The addiction sent me to prison for eight years.

When I got out, I wasn't sure what to do, or who to call. I knew Pastor Rose was raising my kids, and I wasn't sure if I was worthy of breathing the same air as them. I wasn't sure if I would be able to see them at all."

Jimmy paused and looked out into the crowd. Then he continued with his story:

"I called her one day, while I was in a halfway house, and asked her if I could see them. I was never so afraid of rejection in my life. She came through for me. She brought them all the way over to a seedy part of town, just so I could see them"

He stopped again and smiled at his kids. Bo was a strapping young man of 23, and Skyler would be turning 18 in July. They were his world.

"I owe everything I have to Rose England. She is my savior, my champion. When I thought I wasn't worthy of love, she showed me different. I was a convict, but she opened her heart and her home to me. She told me I was a part of her family."

Jimmy was trying hard not to cry, and his voice was cracking with emotion, as he determinedly told his story. He was incredibly humbled by the way she'd forgiven him.

"Folks, I have to tell you this. If you gave me a million dollars, it would not have made me feel as rich as the acceptance of this woman has made me feel. To have been given love, and compassion was one of the greatest gifts I have ever received. I can never repay her. I will always be grateful. Thank you, Rose."

Jimmy ducked his head a moment, steadying himself. He looked up, nodded and stepped down from the podium. The congregation stood up with a standing ovation. The applause lasted more than a minute. His was a testimony that honored Rose England. She was smiling where she sat, surrounded by all the ones she loved best.

The family gathered tightly around her when it was time to go home. She tried to hide it, but she was frail and weak. The congregation sent her flowers and cards wishing her recovery, but it was not to be.

Rose England passed away a month later. They laid her to rest in the fall of her 65th year. Robert took it hard. He had seven years with her and he was grateful, but after her passing he was like a lost puppy. The once familiar blank look returned, and the old farmhouse felt drafty without her warmth.

The family remained in touch with Emily. She'd stayed at the compound when Rose passed away. She took Skyler under her wing and the two planned a trip to Florida soon.

Skyler was attending college, where she was working toward an accounting degree. Robert had a job lined up for her at the station. He was in need of a trustworthy receptionist, as Rhonda Stiles had been fired for revealing classified information to the press.

Bo came into the kitchen one bright sunny day, where Sky was making stew.

"I have some great news, Sky."

"Oh? Spill it." She stopped chopping potatoes, turning to give her brother her attention.

"Well, I'm getting married." Skyler's eyes grew big and round.

"What? Oh my goodness, Bo, I'm so happy for you!"

"Well, there's a little more…Cindy's pregnant."

Sky just stood there staring at him. Finally, she found her voice.

"You're getting married, and having a baby?"

"Yes ma'am, we are."

"Oh my gosh, Bo! Congratulations, I'm so excited for you both. When are you going to do it? Where? Who?"

"Settle down a minute. Now, you know Cindy's dad's a Reverend. He's consented to perform the ceremony. We want something real simple, and we were hoping to have it right here at the compound. What do you think?"

"Oh yes, that's perfect. We can do something like Grandma and Robert did. Oh Bo, she would have been so happy to hear this."

"I know. I sure wish she were here. Listen, I forgot to tell you something else. If it's a girl, we're naming her Rose Marie, after Grandma. If it's a boy, we'll call it James William, after both of our dad's.

"She would have loved those names." Skyler was smiling from ear to ear. She was murmuring to her self long after Bo left, "A wedding and a baby, how wonderful."

The wedding was set for the following month. They planned a casual affair, with only 40 to 50 guests. Bo and Cindy Conrad were expecting a baby in the summer. It was an exciting time, as they readied their little ranch house in town for the new arrival.

They were all zooming around now with the wedding plans. Two more days and they were still arranging flowers all along the fence line. The ceremony would be performed in the gazebo that Rose loved so much.

It was time. Bo stood out on the lawn watching for his bride. The music had started, and he was ready. The guests were seated in white chairs set to face the gazebo. White roses were placed all along the opening and they were made into a chain and draped gracefully around the parameter of the seating area.

Cindy came through the doors and everyone stood. The music was soft as the bride came toward her groom. On her wrist, she wore a golden bangle that belonged to Rose. It was her way of remembering her on this day.

Skyler sat between her mother and father in the front row. Robert sat just beyond them. They felt a breeze blowing over the lake today, and the flowers flitted back and forth. They all knew Rose was with them. This was her favorite place in the entire world.

It was a month after the wedding, when Annie and Jimmy sat everyone down. They had an announcement. They were going to Colombia to be missionaries. It was a calling for them, a calling they were excited to answer.

.er knew her grandmother would have been thrilled to
﹢ news. She'd hoped Jimmy would continue to lead worship
church, but this was a very big development. Annie and Jimmy
﹢ a team. They were very happy together these days; who knew,
aybe they would finally become Mr. and Mrs.

At the police station, Skyler was near Robert daily. They all wanted him to retire and travel, but he was content to continue policing the community. As long as they kept voting for him to be the chief, he would serve and protect.

Skyler would awaken on occasion and she still had visions that needed to be heeded.

Robert was heading to the courthouse one sunny day when Skyler called him. A gunshot woke her abruptly from a nap. It was happening quickly, like a movie in fast motion. She was disoriented and shook her head to clear the blurry images.

The smoky gray form of a gunman started to materialize. She saw the great steps as he proceeded towards the enormous brick building and knew what was going to happen.

Skyler said a silent prayer that she could reach him, as she desperately dialed Robert's number. He answered, and she told him there was going to be a shooting in the courthouse today. She told him it was a young man in his early twenties. He was Caucasian, and wearing a blue jean jacket and black pants.

Robert held an emergency briefing. The security team decided to screen all entrants to the courthouse that afternoon, effective immediately. They set up a checkpoint outside the building. Sure enough, a young man was stopped and as they patted him down, a revolver was discovered in a hidden pocket inside of his jacket.

He was arrested and detained. The story he gave was that the judge was crooked and needed to die. It was chilling to think he could have gotten through the checkpoint and been allowed access to the courtroom. His intent was murder.

Through the years word traveled, about Skyler Conrad's gift. She was set upon many times by the local newspaper. Robert always said, "No comment," when asked about her eerie warnings, but he couldn't stop reporters from asking her for interviews.

Skyler would go to work, then return to the sanctity of the house in the hills. She still had Matilda, who was now a little old lady. It was a good thing Skyler had a warning system dwelling inside, as Matilda was almost completely deaf and blind.

Sometimes she'd be sleeping and her eyes would fly open if someone was coming. It was usually Bo, or Cindy and the baby. Sometimes, Robert would just be cruising up and around, perusing the area, keeping his promise to Rose that he would watch over her kids.

Annie and Jimmy were traveling back to the states frequently. They were determined to be near and present for their family, as well as do the work they loved. The life they chose as missionaries in a third world country had opened their eyes to the blessings they had been privileged with for the last thirty years. They were giving back now.

In memory of Rose, they built a church in Colombia, and called it "Rivers Edge." Her portrait hung in the main hallway, a tribute to her, for giving them both the inspiration to serve others.

The compound was Skyler's world. She tended the garden and cared for her grandmother's roses. Sometimes, she just sat out in the gazebo, reading a book, with the old comforter Rose loved, wrapped around her.

She received a letter from Terry Samuels one day. He'd finally gotten out of prison. In the letter, he thanked her for being an inspiration to him to stay clean and remain free. He told her both of his girls had graduated from high school. He was thrilled that Cassie was engaged. He would have the honor of walking her down the isle.

It was a new beginning for him, and he went on to tell her he never forgot how sweet and accepting she was. She changed his life. Skyler smiled as she lay the letter down. So many years ago, so much had happened.

She rocked in the old porch swing that evening, sipping cocoa. Matilda was happily perched on her lap. She knew she was blessed. God had given her such an amazing life, and she had a great family. She thought about maybe writing a book. Her grandmother always wrote in a journal. Sky never had, but maybe now was a good time to start. She would purchase a notebook next time she was in town.

It was a glorious spring day, and Skyler was babysitting for Bo and Cindy. As she tickled her 18-month-old niece, she noticed a peculiar brightness in little Rosie's eyes. They shone brilliantly, and seemed to be lit from somewhere within. Skyler studied them, thinking, *could it be?* She closed her eyes, then opened them to gaze once more into the bright eyes of Rosie. She silently asked herself if it was possible. Her grandmother's spirit seemed to be staring back at her, or was it just a trick of the light?

The baby giggled and squealed as Skyler bounced her some more, tickling and kissing her fat pink cheeks. Tomorrow, she might have to make a call. For now, she just crooned to the child, "We're going to see what's up with those eyes of yours, aren't we Rosie? Yes, we are."

She knew there was only one person to call. That person was Emily Stone. Emily would tell her what she needed to know.

The End